She seemed frozen to the spot

Caine found himself staring into her wide emerald eyes. He had the strangest sensation. If he took a step closer, he'd drown in them. Feeling the uneven pattern of his heart, he paused on the brink, then pulled himself back. Shaken, he turned away.

As the door closed behind him, Ivy exhaled the breath she had been unconsciously holding. She hadn't just imagined that one electric moment. Even though they hadn't touched, she was still reeling from the intimate contact.

She stared dreamlike into the flames. There was something dangerous about Caine. There was a simmering anger in his eyes. Enraged, he would be ruthless. His kisses wouldn't be friendly. His touch wouldn't be tender or familiar. And, she knew, she wouldn't be able to easily turn away from him.

Dear Reader,

Although our culture is always changing, the desire to love and be loved is a constant in every woman's heart. Silhouette Romances reflect that desire, sweeping you away with books that will make you laugh and cry, poignant stories that will move you time and time again.

This year we're featuring Romances with a playful twist. Remember those fun-loving heroines who always manage to get themselves into tricky predicaments? You'll enjoy reading about their escapades in Silhouette Romances by Brittany Young, Debbie Macomber, Annette Broadrick and Rita Rainville.

We're also publishing Romances by many of your all-time favorites such as Ginna Gray, Dixie Browning, Laurie Paige and Joan Hohl. Your overwhelming reaction to these authors has served as a touchstone for us, and we're pleased to bring you more books with Silhouette's distinctive medley of charm, wit and—above all—*romance*. I hope you enjoy this book, and the many stories to come.

Sincerely,

Rosalind Noonan
Senior Editor
SILHOUETTE BOOKS

RUTH LANGAN
Family
Secrets

Silhouette **Romance**

Published by Silhouette Books New York

America's Publisher of Contemporary Romance

To Patrick,
with love

SILHOUETTE BOOKS
300 E. 42nd St., New York, N.Y. 10017

Copyright © 1986 by Ruth Langan

Distributed by Pocket Books

ISBN: 0-373-08407-2

First Silhouette Books printing January 1986

10 9 8 7 6 5 4 3 2 1

America's Publisher of Contemporary Romance

Printed in the U.S.A.

RUTH LANGAN

enjoys writing about modern men and women who are not afraid to be both strong and tender. Her sense of humor is evident in her work. Happily married to her childhood sweetheart, she thrives on the chaos created by two careers and five children.

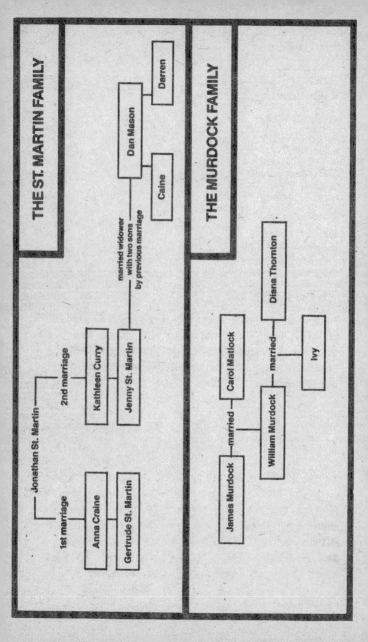

THE ST. MARTIN FAMILY

Jonathan St. Martin

1st marriage

Anna Craine

Gertrude St. Martin

2nd marriage

Kathleen Curry

Jenny St. Martin

married widower with two sons by previous marriage

Dan Mason

Caine

Darren

THE MURDOCK FAMILY

James Murdock —married— Carol Matlock

William Murdock —married— Diana Thornton

Ivy

Prologue

> There is something shocking in your past that you have never revealed. I wonder just how much you'll be willing to pay to buy my silence?

At the words in the letter, Gertrude St. Martin's eyes rounded in horror. Her legs, she discovered, had turned to rubber. Clutching the arm of the chair, she staggered, then sank down heavily. Her mind reeled from the force of the blow. All her life she had carried this burden in her heart. The pain of it had diminished through the years but had never completely left her. It didn't seem possible that anyone alive today could know of that incident in her youth. The past had been buried. Dead and buried. Or had it?

Chapter One

"Miss St. Martin. Your nephew, Caine."

Forgetting propriety, Gertrude rushed across the room.

"I'm so glad you got here before the others, Caine. I was hoping we could spend a little time together— alone."

Strong arms wrapped the old woman in a bear hug. She leaned against him, absorbing his quiet strength.

Taking his face in her hands, she hungrily studied his craggy features. Caine had always been the dark and somber one, the quiet one, the loner. Thick shaggy hair was always in need of a trim. Long sooty lashes ringed piercing gray eyes. A threadbare sweater topped narrow jeans, which rode low on his hips. His casual attire belied his success as an architect.

A smile softened the old woman's features. Then, seeming to catch herself, she fell into a familiar gruff pattern with which they were both more comfortable.

"You look frazzled. Are you sure you're taking care of yourself?"

He frowned, and she remembered the serious, thoughtful child he had been. "I've had a lot on my mind lately."

At her look of concern he seemed to catch himself. He chuckled, a warm, vibrant sound, and gave her another hug before releasing her. "Too much fast living. I've been dividing my time between New York and Arizona. But the Arizona project is nearly finished now. I'll be relieved to settle down in New York for the rest of the year. That is, unless the European project is approved. Then I'll be commuting across continents."

"Oh, Caine." She sighed heavily. "Your life is entirely too fast-paced. I'd hoped you could spend an occasional long weekend here with me. I've missed you. You and Darren." She brightened. "I'd even hoped you might finally start the renovation of the cottage."

He nodded. "You know how much I've always loved it, Trudy. As long as you're agreeable, I think it would be a challenge. I don't see why I couldn't fit it into my schedule this year."

"I'd love having you here. And the caretaker's cottage has been vacant too long." Some of the tension seemed to drain from her. "We must celebrate."

Caine watched as his aunt strode to the cabinet and poured two tumblers of her favorite aged whiskey.

Turning, she handed one to him and touched his glass with hers. In two quick gulps she downed her drink.

"Keeps the blood flowing," she stated in that sharp, staccato voice that never wavered with age. Glancing at her watch, she said, "Darren's plane should be in soon. Did I mention that I'd invited Ivy to my birthday celebration?"

"Ivy Murdock?"

She nodded. Her voice lowered a fraction. "And her mother."

At the sudden silence in the room, the wrinkled folds of the old woman's face turned into a guileless smile. "Oh, dear. I see I did forget to mention that."

Caine swallowed back the remark that sprang to his lips. Even at eighty, Gertrude St. Martin rarely forgot anything. "You conniving old matchmaker," he said with a grin.

Gertrude walked to the fireplace and held her hands toward the blaze. She was tall, nearly as tall as Caine's six feet, and her carriage was still erect. Her hair was steel gray, which accentuated sparkling blue eyes.

"I know Ivy seems a bit scattered, but she's a dear. I want to see her again. I've missed her. Even though we're not blood-related, the three of you grew up here."

"You don't need to explain." Caine drank, feeling the warmth snake through his veins. He finished his drink and set down the crystal tumbler before meeting her look. "I was only thinking of Darren. He might find Ivy's presence awkward, with his separation from his wife so fresh. But you're right, of course. Ivy is as much family as the rest of us. And it's your birthday, Trudy. I think you should surround your-self with people you enjoy."

"Well said. Besides—" her eyes twinkled with a hint of mischief "—who said anything about Darren? Maybe it's you I'm planning as Ivy's escort for the weekend."

Caine winced. "When you are going to accept the fact that I'm a confirmed bachelor? I like the single life."

"That's only because you haven't tried marriage." She sniffed.

"Is the pot calling the kettle black? The last I heard, you were still Miss St. Martin."

"That's different. I'm too old to change."

"We're two of a kind, Trudy. That's why we get along so well."

Those words were so typical of Caine, the old woman thought as she looked at him. There was a bond of deep affection between them. He would have given her the moon if he could, but all she'd ever wanted from either of her nephews was their love.

"Well, I'm not trying to marry you off. But there's nothing wrong with a little feminine companionship when you're not working."

Caine watched as the old woman lifted the bottle, considered for a long moment, then replaced the stopper and returned it to its place on the shelf. With the exaggerated sigh of a martyr she turned away, mumbling, "Fool doctors. Don't know what's good for a healthy body."

Caine smiled. "That never stopped you before." To change the subject, he said, "I can't recall that you ever celebrated a birthday before. In fact, you used to say you hated birthdays. They were a reminder that you were growing older. Why this sudden desire for a big party? Is there something you haven't told me?''

He noticed a slight trembling of her hand. She was definitely agitated, but he couldn't figure out why. At her silence, he muttered, ''Okay. What are you up to, Trudy?''

She gave him what she hoped was a pained expression. ''Me? Up to? Now that's a fine thing.''

''Out with it.'' He caught her by the shoulders and turned her toward him. ''Something's bothering you. Now tell me.''

She bit her lip, then looked up into his dark eyes. ''I think it's just the isolation here. I didn't get into the city at all this winter. I get a little jumpy.''

''With Chester and all the servants?'' His look hardened. ''What are you keeping from me?''

She glanced down. ''I'm just edgy, Caine. Strangers sometimes wander onto the grounds. With all the talk of crime and criminals, there's no telling who's lurking about these days.''

His eyes narrowed. ''Have any of the buildings been broken into? Have you been robbed?''

''No. Nothing like that.'' She turned from his probing look. ''I'm just glad you're here, Caine. That's all.''

Caine watched her for long silent moments. It wasn't like his aunt to be so uneasy. He intended to make it a point to speak to Chester and the servants. And to make some security arrangements before he went back to the city.

The motorcycle skimmed across the ruts in the road and veered sharply at the opening in the gate. Here the pavement of the long winding driveway was freshly resurfaced, as smooth as the water on the duck pond that was visible from the entrance to the wooded estate.

Ivy Murdock smiled at the sight of a pair of ducks making lazy circles in the glassy surface of the water. Their annual return was a ritual that signaled the arrival of springtime. Once again, they had made it home.

Home. Was it possible for her to return, too? Even though this fabulous estate of Gertrude St. Martin had never really belonged to Ivy, it was the only place that had ever felt like home. She glanced at the magnificent house on the hill.

Thoughts and images tumbled over one another in her mind. The first time Ivy had seen this beautiful setting, she'd felt as if she had found heaven. Despite her mother's resentment at what she considered a menial position, Ivy and her father were happier here than they'd ever been. She'd missed this place, these people, with an ache that was almost physical. Those first years away at college had been the hardest of her life. But the pain had been softened by frequent visits home. After her father was gone and her mother took a small apartment in the city, there had no longer been a home. Alone, drifting, her art became her anchor. She'd painted constantly, day and night, to ease the loneliness, until finally she'd made a niche for herself in the impersonal city.

Her heart fluttered as she drove nearer. Her hands inside the leather gloves grew moist. Why had she accepted this invitation? She nearly laughed at the word. An invitation from Gertrude St. Martin was really a royal command. And she'd accepted for a very simple reason. She wanted to see Aunt Tru again. She wanted to be surrounded, if only for a few days, by the family and the life of luxury that had always eluded her.

Though her father had only been an employee, she'd felt drawn to the St. Martin past as if it were her own. The lives of the St. Martins had been interwoven into the fabric of hers.

Her throat felt dry. Revving the engine, Ivy took the last curve of the driveway at breakneck speed.

She strode beneath a covered portico and glanced around the long-remembered estate. She felt a sense of joy at the sheer beauty of it. The house, of weathered brick and stone, rose to three stories amid five hundred prime acres of wooded rolling hills in upstate New York. The building didn't intrude on the beautiful setting, it enhanced it. The house blended into the rolling landscape as naturally as the sunset. The mile-long driveway offered a view of carefully cultivated lawns and gardens. The caretaker's cottage, just beyond the gate house, appeared vacant now. A lump formed in her throat; the estate had been her home for eight years.

The drive from New York City had been made in just over three hours. She shivered as the sun passed beneath the clouds. Although the spring air still held the chill of winter, the bright sunshine had made the ride tolerable.

Caine hurriedly rounded the corner of the house and stood watching as the helmeted figure walked briskly toward the door. The driver was tall and slender and wore a gray leather jacket. Faded jeans were stuffed into tall gray leather boots. The stride was purposeful, as if the stranger knew exactly where to go. Was this the sort of intruder who had been frightening his aunt?

Without warning, a rough hand caught at Ivy's shoulder, spinning her around. She was hauled against a solid wall of chest and nearly lifted off her feet. Looking up, she found herself staring into dark, stormy eyes beneath slanted black brows. The scowling face masked a carefully contained fury.

"I hope you're here by accident. The county road is a mile back that way." He nodded toward the road. "You're on private property."

"Take your hands off me." The voice, muffled behind the helmet, was deep, sultry.

His eyes widened in surprise and his grip tightened. The flesh beneath the leather was surprisingly soft. The figure struggled, twisting against his broad chest.

One hand broke free and raised to the helmet, ripping it off. A mass of dark hair, the color of the night sky, tumbled over her shoulders and down her back in a riot of waves. Caine was thunderstruck at the sight of her.

She was stunning. In her anger, green eyes flashed. The lashes were thick and dark, casting little shadows on high cheekbones. The face was oval, delicate, with flawless skin, and lips pursed in a little pout. He tried to ignore the hypnotic floral scent of her perfume which mingled with the spring breeze. Staring down into her face, he felt a strong, instantaneous attraction that startled him with its intensity.

"Who the hell are you? And what are you doing here?"

She glowered at him. "I'm not answering any of your questions until you take your hands off me."

He continued to hold her.

"You're hurting me."

He withdrew the offending hand.

She stepped back a pace. Her voice had a breathless quality. "My name is Ivy Murdock. And I was invited here for the weekend."

"Ivy? My God!" Caine studied the slender figure before allowing a small smile to cross his lips.

Though he'd been away at college when her family had moved to the estate, he had seen her a few times during her childhood. She'd always reminded him of a frisky colt, running wild and free, climbing trees or dashing across the hills. Yes, he thought, his eyes narrowing. Although the braces were gone, and the hair was longer and darker now, she was still the free spirit he had glimpsed in years past.

"Hello, Weed. I'm sorry I didn't recognize you. I'm Caine St. Martin. I see you've finally quit growing."

Now it was her turn to be caught off guard. In her surprise and anger, she hadn't recognized the man in the careless attire as the college student she had studiously avoided in her youth. Thick dark hair spilled over a wide forehead. The face was older now, and if possible, even more handsome, in a rugged, craggy way. His shoulders were wide, the muscles of his forearms bulging beneath the sweater. The hands that had pinned her were strong, work-worn. She could still feel the imprint of his fingers on her skin.

She flushed at the hateful nickname he'd tagged on her years ago, when she had grown taller and faster than any of her classmates. Weed. Even then he'd towered over her. And, she remembered, she'd vowed that one day she would cut him down to size. "So have you."

His gaze roamed over her slender figure.

She gave him a quick, contemptuous glare, then punched the doorbell. "Thanks for the warm reception. Do you intend to greet all your aunt's guests like this, or was I the only lucky one?"

A hint of a smile touched Caine's lips. It was a good thing he'd let go of her. He hadn't known he was holding a tiger.

The door opened. A ruddy-faced man with a thatch of rusty hair liberally sprinkled with silver stood at attention.

"Chester. Oh, I'm so glad to see you."

"Oh, my. Our little Miss Ivy." His smile grew.

Little? She nearly laughed at his words. At five feet eight inches, she was at least four inches taller than this dear sweet man.

His cherubic face was wreathed in smiles. "Come in, lass. Come in."

Ignoring the scowling man behind her, she gave Chester an impulsive hug, which he accepted awkwardly before glancing at Caine and stepping back a pace.

Chester straightened his jacket and brushed invisible lint from his lapel while his cheeks turned crimson. "Miss St. Martin is upstairs in the sitting room."

She laughed, a joyful sound in the silence of the huge marbled foyer. "Thanks, Chester."

As she turned away, he cleared his throat. "Miss Ivy."

She paused. "Yes?"

"I'll need your keys. To park that—thing in the garage."

She grinned. "Okay." Rummaging through her pockets, she shrugged. "I don't seem to have them. Maybe I..." She went back outside to check the ignition. With a puzzled frown she muttered, "Now where did I..."

Chester pointed to the ground. In the scuffle, she must have dropped them.

With a grin, she retrieved the keys and handed them to him. "Here, Chester. Think you can handle it?"

Caine bit back the laughter at the look on the butler's face. For a moment Chester stared at the motorcycle as if it were a space vehicle. Then he squared his shoulders. "I guess if you can drive it all the way from New York City, I can manage to drive it a hundred yards."

Caine took pity on the old man. "Never mind, Chester. I'll take care of Miss Murdock's motorcycle."

The butler shot him a lot of gratitude. "What will I do with this helmet?" He held it stiffly away from him, unwilling to allow it to contaminate his spotless white shirt.

"Leave it with the bike. That way I can find it when I need it." She started toward the stairs.

"Miss Ivy."

She paused.

"Your glove." He bent and lifted it from the doorway.

She glanced at the single glove in her hand, gave a wry grin, then walked back and took the other from the butler.

"Thanks, Chester."

"Now, if you'll just follow me, I'll announce you."

Caine chuckled as she took the stairs two at a time. She might be older, and if possible even prettier, but she hadn't changed a bit. She was still a lovable scatterbrain.

"Miss Ivy Murdock."

Ivy couldn't help laughing at Chester's pompous tones. He was the most wonderful stuffed shirt. She squeezed his arm and in a stage whisper muttered, "You did that just fine, Chester. Just like in the movies."

A flush stained his throat and crept upward from his starched collar to his cheeks.

"Ivy. Dear Ivy." Gertrude had hurriedly seated herself in a tall wing chair, her hands regally gripping the armrests. The dusty rose silk of her dress swirled about her ankles. At her throat rested an antique cameo broach pinned to a scarlet velvet ribbon.

Coming into the room, Caine leaned a hip against the windowsill and watched in amusement as his aunt played the role of queen to perfection.

"Aunt Tru."

Ivy rushed across the room and kissed her cheek, then gave her a warm embrace.

The old woman allowed her gaze to travel over the slender figure before her. "Is that what they're wearing this year in the big city?"

Ivy laughed and pressed a cheek to the old woman's forehead. "You're wearing enough finery for both of us. You look wonderful."

"Was that a cement mixer you drove?"

"A bike."

"Bike?"

"Motorcycle."

"It sounded like a garbage truck. Why on earth don't you drive a car like everyone else?"

"New York streets are too congested. With a motorcycle, I can sneak around traffic. It's the only way to survive midtown Manhattan."

"Ummm." Gertrude's features remained stiff, but the look in her eyes warmed. "Have you said hello to my nephew yet?"

Caine watched Ivy stiffen.

"Oh, yes. We've had an interesting reunion."

Even in anger, her face was exquisite. In the dappled sunlight of late afternoon, her face was a mixture of light and shadow. Her eyes were so much greener than he'd remembered. So green they'd put his aunt's antique emeralds to shame. She hadn't bothered to run a comb through her hair. Dark, burnished, it fell in artless disarray about her face and shoulders. Even here, across the room, he could remember the delicate floral scent of her perfume.

Seeing her frown, Caine returned a lazy smile of his own.

Ivy's heart tumbled as he continued to stare at her.

"Well," Aunt Tru said to break the tension. "Beneath those tacky clothes, I can see that you've grown into a lovely young woman. And I'm glad you were able to make it for my birthday party."

"I wouldn't have missed it. How are you feeling, Aunt Tru?"

"Fit as a fiddle. Tomorrow night I'm going to dance until dawn. Now, come sit beside me and tell me about your life in the big city."

The young woman grinned and began to pull a chair across the floor. As she turned, she nearly collided with a mirrored pedestal holding an exquisite bronze bust. Instantly Caine steadied it and took the chair from her hands. With ease he set it beside his aunt. Their eyes met briefly and Ivy saw the glint of humor in his dark depths.

"Still knocking into things, I see."

"Still preventing disasters, I see."

He was laughing at her. He had always laughed at her. She knew she was absentminded. But Caine's presence seemed to make things worse.

While she sat down, Caine added another log to the fire. With his back to her, he luxuriated in her deep, throaty voice.

"There isn't much to tell. I spend every day painting. On weekends, when the city quiets down a bit, I come out of my seclusion to shop, see the sights, take in a play or concert."

"Seclusion. Huh. You're much too young to be living like a hermit."

Ivy chuckled. "I'm not a hermit, Aunt Tru. I'm an artist."

"So is Caine. Well—" she shrugged at Ivy's look of surprise "—an architect. They're practically the same thing. And he leads an entirely too fast-paced life. You should each take a lesson from the other."

Ivy chose to ignore Gertrude's comment. "Though I need a lot of privacy for my work, I've made some friends in the city. But actually I often prefer my own company. I'd rather be alone than have to put up with silly, useless chatter."

The old woman nodded, pleased with that remark. She had lived by pretty much the same philosophy throughout her own life.

"Caine. Stop poking at the fire and come join us. And bring that bottle of whiskey," she added as an afterthought. "We'll drink to Ivy's arrival."

"You'd drink to anything, Aunt Trudy," he teased. "I've had my limit. And you have, too. Don't you always take a nap before dinner?"

"A nap?" She scoffed. "I may take a walk, but I have no intention of lying down. I—I don't sleep well these days."

Ivy saw the look of surprise that crossed Caine's face at his aunt's words. "In all the years I've known you, you were always such a sound sleeper, Aunt Trudy."

"Well, lately I've been restless. Now come over here and join us." The tone of her voice rang with authority. "And bring that bottle."

Caine shrugged. If she'd managed to live by her own rules for eighty years, who was he to try to change her now? He filled three glasses, then sat down beside Ivy.

Warmed by the fire, Ivy removed the leather jacket and dropped it on the back of her chair. As Gertrude lifted her glass in a toast, Caine's gaze slid over Ivy.

Beneath the jacket, the silk shirt was hand painted and obviously expensive. It draped gracefully over high, firm breasts, then tapered to a narrow waist. Her jeans were faded and even bore smudges of paint. They fit over her slim hips and long legs like a second skin. Her watch, he noted, was inexpensive and practical. The ruby and diamond ring on her little finger, however, bore the exquisite markings of a fine craftsman. Everything about Ivy Murdock seemed to be a contradiction.

Draining her glass, the old woman said, "Tell us about your exhibit, Ivy. I'd planned to attend, but the winter storms kept us housebound for weeks. Chester wouldn't venture any farther than the little store on Sumner Road."

"The exhibit was held at the Norton Gallery." As the first fiery drops of liquid warmed Ivy's blood, she felt Caine's brooding gaze. She blamed the liquor for the heat that stained her cheeks.

Caine nodded his appreciation. "The Norton's one of the best. You can't get much higher, unless you make it to the museum."

Ivy smiled almost shyly, suddenly warmed by his words. "It was a thrill. The reviews were very kind."

Gertrude watched Ivy's reaction to Caine with intense interest. "Kind. They were absolutely raving about you."

"You read them?" Ivy looked pleased.

"Of course I did. Caine mailed me a copy of every New York paper that carried a review."

Ivy glanced at him in surprise. "Thank you." Turning to Gertrude, she added, "I would have sent them myself, but I was afraid you'd think I was bragging."

The old woman placed a soft, blue-veined hand over Ivy's. "You should be bragging. You have a wonderful talent. It's something to boast about. In fact, I do a little bragging myself. Everyone in this county knows about Ivy Murdock's success."

"I suppose it's because of the success of that exhibit that I've been given a new commission," Ivy confided. "The Blayfield Building. I'm to do a mural in the main lobby, and several of my paintings will hang in the executive lounge."

Gertrude cast a quizzical glance at Caine before turning to Ivy. "The Blayfield Building? That's a wonderful opportunity. Your art will be seen by thousands."

Ivy beamed. "I'm thrilled at the chance. I'm already working on the paintings. I won't be able to start the mural until the building is constructed, sometime next year. But I can already see it in my mind."

"I think," Gertrude said, leaning back in her chair with a smug look, "that you're going to be a very famous artist one day."

Ivy stared at the amber liquid in her glass. Her voice was subdued. "I'll settle for good. I want to be a good artist, Aunt Tru. Not a famous one."

The old woman nodded her approval. Clearing her throat, she said, "Did your mother tell you she was invited to my party?"

Something flickered across Ivy's face. When she spoke, her voice was low. "No, she didn't. Will she be here today?"

"No. She said she'd be driving up tomorrow in plenty of time for the party tomorrow night. But Darren should be here any time now."

At a knock on the door, all three looked up. The butler paused in the doorway. "Flowers have arrived for you, Miss St. Martin."

"Oh, how lovely. Tell Martha to bring them up to my bedroom suite." Gertrude stood. "I want to see the flowers before I take my evening stroll." Her gaze swept Ivy. "You did bring something besides those awful blue jeans, didn't you?"

Ivy chuckled. "I threw a few things in a bag." Her smile faded. She jumped up. "Oh. I forgot. It's on the back of my bike."

"Never mind. I'll have Chester retrieve it." The old woman arched an eyebrow. "And I'll have Martha see that they're neatly pressed before hanging them in your room."

"That isn't necessary, Aunt Tru."

The old woman paused in the doorway. "They've just spent the better part of the day tied on the back of a motorcycle." The haughty tone of her voice spoke volumes. "Martha will see to them."

When the door closed, Ivy and Caine stared at each other wordlessly, then burst into laughter.

Caine shook his head. "She means business. You know she'll have her way."

Ivy nodded. "Hasn't she always? She's the strongest woman I've ever known."

"And you, Ivy. Aren't you strong?"

She shrugged. "Strong enough to get by."

"You seem to have done more than just get by." He'd been impressed by the talent he'd seen at her New York exhibit. In all of her paintings he'd sensed an underlying quiet strength.

Uncomfortable under his gaze, she stood and began to prowl the room, touching familiar old objects.

Even when she was young, she'd been puzzled by Caine's dark, serious nature. Darren had always known how to make her laugh, to make small talk or be silly enough to put her at ease. But Caine would often remain silent in her presence, unless he had something important to say.

At twenty-five, she found herself in the company of artists and critics, reporters and art dealers. She had poise and self-confidence. She was bright and articulate. But Caine, only seven years her senior, still made her feel like an awkward teenager.

"I get the feeling you aren't exactly pleased that your aunt is having this party, Caine." She looked up. "Or is it the guest list that bothers you?"

He shook a cigarette from the pack and held a lighter to it. Through a haze of smoke, he said, "I'm just a little puzzled by it. Aren't you a little curious about her behavior? She seems nervous. And it isn't like Aunt Trudy to make a fuss over her birthday."

"She's eighty years old, Caine. Maybe she's feeling lonely. Or nostalgic. Maybe she wants to recapture her youth. Whatever the reason, I think it's sweet that she invited us."

"How did you think she looked?"

Ivy paused. "She doesn't seem to have aged a bit. Her mind seems as alert as ever. Her eyesight is perfect. She doesn't miss much. And her tongue is as sharp as I remember."

Caine heard the note of affection in her tone. "You really like her, don't you?"

Ivy felt a surge of warmth at the thought of the old woman. "She was always so good to me. Despite her tough veneer, she was one friend I could count on. When my father's health began to fail, it was Aunt Tru I turned to. When I needed money for college, she helped me find a job near the campus. And when I begged my father to allow me to study art, it was Aunt Tru who persuaded him that art was as necessary to me as breathing." Ivy's eyes took on a faraway look. "My mother had him convinced I'd never be anything but a starving artist living in some unheated hovel in the Village."

Caine heard the tremor in her voice for that one unguarded moment.

Ivy turned away from his scrutiny and lifted a piece of sculpture to the light.

Caine walked to the fireplace and stared at the flames. With a flick of the wrist, he tossed the cigarette in the fire. Turning, he said, "I know Trudy too well. She's up to something."

"I think that's an awful thing to say. Why can't you simply let her have her fun?"

He took a step closer, towering over her. "Contrary to what you may think of me, Ivy, I have no objection to—" his lips curled into a smile "—fun. I've been known to laugh a time or two myself."

"You could have fooled me." Her eyes widened as the sculpture she was holding slipped from her grasp. In one swift motion, Caine caught it before it crashed to the floor. He replaced it gently on the table.

Ivy froze, reacting to both the suddenness of the near-accident and Caine's swift response. Caine found himself staring into her wide emerald eyes. He had the strange feeling that if he took a step closer, he'd drown in them. His hands would find their way into that wild tangle of hair. And his lips would taste the most inviting mouth he'd every imagined.

His eyes narrowed slightly. He needed only to take one step. Feeling the uneven pattern of his heart, he paused on the brink, then pulled himself back. Shaken, he turned away.

"I'll see you at dinner."

As the door closed behind him, Ivy exhaled the breath she had been unconsciously holding. She hadn't imagined that one electric moment. Even though they hadn't touched, she was still reeling from the intimate contact.

She stared dreamlike into the flames. There was something dangerous about Caine. Though he could be kind and considerate of his aunt, Ivy had felt the sting of his anger. She touched her fingertips to her shoulders, remembering how roughly he had held her when he'd thought she was an intruder. There had been a simmering anger in his eyes. Enraged, he could be ruthless. His kisses wouldn't be friendly. His touch wouldn't be tender or familiar. And, she knew, she wouldn't be able to easily turn away from him.

Annoyed with her thoughts, she opened the door and started down the hallway in search of the maid. Where would Martha have put her bag?

Chapter Two

Ivy stood at the upstairs window and watched Gertrude's tall figure stride along the driveway toward the house. The old woman had been gone for more than an hour. She must have walked several miles.

She had the gait of a woman half her age and moved with the ramrod stance of a drill sergeant. Dressed in warm tweeds, with a jaunty cap perched on her white hair, she was the picture of robust health.

Across the hills, the fading sun slanted ribbons of shadow and light through the trees. Ivy marveled at the sounds of silence, alien to her after her years in the city. Even this house seemed steeped in silence. She'd actually heard Martha's starched skirts swish as she went about her work in the thickly carpeted hallway outside Ivy's room.

She glanced impatiently at her watch. Where was the maid with her clothes? She should have insisted on taking care of her own things. If they weren't brought up to her room in the next few minutes, she would go in search of them.

Gertrude stepped vigorously up the driveway to the front door. Before she could knock, the butler swung the door open. Handing her the mail, he said, "Your nephew, Darren, arrived, Miss St. Martin. He's up in his room. And your lawyers, Mr. Tisdale and young Mr. Tisdale, are here, too. I gave them rooms in the north suite, as you requested."

"Thank you, Chester."

"Their luggage has been delivered to their rooms. The maids are unpacking it now. If you don't need me for anything else, I'll see to parking their cars."

"Fine." Distracted, she waved him away and headed toward the stairs as she sorted through the mail. When she came to a familiar, plain white envelope, her heart stopped. She dropped the rest of the mail in her eagerness to open it. Envelopes and cards floated down, fluttering about her feet like dry leaves.

With trembling fingers she pulled the folded note from its envelope and read the carefully pasted words.

Your past has come back to haunt you. Some of your party guests may turn out to be much more than they appear. I think it's time for us to discuss a fee for my silence. Watch for my next note. It will be most important.

"Oh, no."

The words on the page blurred. The old woman felt a buzzing in her ears as if from a great swarm of bees. The letter fell from her hands. The stairs in front of her seemed to waver, then fall away from her. She crumpled to the floor.

Ivy was tired of waiting for the maid. All she wanted was to soak in a nice warm tub, and then dress for dinner. But first she needed her clothes. As she opened her bedroom door and started down the hallway, she heard Gertrude's muffled exclamation, followed by a muted thump.

From the top of the stairs, she saw the limp form of the old woman sprawled facedown below her. In an instant she was at her side.

"Aunt Tru." She rolled the heavy form over and felt for a pulse at her throat. Relieved to find her alive, she began loosening the buttons at her neck.

"Chester. Chester." Frantically kneeling over the prone figure, she vigorously rubbed the cold hands.

Relief flooded through Ivy at the sight of Caine at the top of the stairs. As he rushed to them, she called "Hurry, Caine. I don't know what's happened."

The front door opened. The butler ran to them, then, seeing Miss St. Martin's unconscious form, he hurried to the phone. "I'll call her doctor."

"Chester, is she taking any medication?" Caine touched a hand to Trudy's forehead.

"Not that I know of," the butler called as he dialed the number.

While Ivy and Caine rubbed her hands, a little color began returning to Trudy's ashen face. Her lids fluttered open and she stared wordlessly from one to the other.

"Thank goodness. Aunt Tru, what happened?"

The old woman stared at Ivy for long moments, then turned to Caine. She could read the concern in their eyes. Looking away, she whispered, "I must have exercised too vigorously. It was nothing. I just fainted."

"People don't faint for no reason," Caine protested.

"I'm old, Caine," she snapped, trying to sit up.

"Sometimes I think you're younger than I am. Now lie still. Chester's calling the doctor."

"No. I won't have it. Chester," she commanded, "hang up that phone this instant."

Confused, the butler glanced at Caine.

"I want the doctor to look at her," Caine ordered.

Chester began to speak into the phone.

"You hang that up, do you hear? And help me to my bed."

"You're not going anywhere until the doctor has a look at you."

Aunt Trudy's voice grew stronger. Her face was pink with rage. "I will not be seen lying on the floor. I insist that you take me to my room."

As Caine lifted her, she turned to Ivy. "And you can retrieve my mail and bring it to me."

Ivy nodded.

While Caine mounted the stairs with his burden, Ivy bent to her task. The letters had scattered all over the foyer floor. One envelope, she noted, had been torn open. Searching for its contents, she spied a paper tucked into a corner under the stairs. She picked it up, straightened, then placed it on top of the other letters. Quickly scooping up the rest of the mail, she hurried to catch up with Caine.

In the elegant master bedroom, Caine lowered his aunt to her bed.

"I don't want you to get up until the doctor has had a chance to examine you. I'd rather not have you fall again."

Gertrude's temper flared. "I won't be treated like some weak old woman."

In his concern for her, his voice hardened. "Downstairs, you wanted to blame this on being old. Now you're resisting it. Make up your mind, Trudy."

Overhearing him, Ivy resented the way he was browbeating his aunt. "Caine."

He turned at the sound of Ivy's voice.

"Here's your aunt's mail. Where would you like me to put it?"

Distractedly running a hand through his hair, he muttered, "I don't care. Anywhere."

"I want it," his aunt commanded.

Something in her tone caught his attention. He took the mail from Ivy's hands and began to hand it to Gertrude. His gaze fell on the opened letter on the top of the pile. Turning away, he scanned the strange message. His puzzled look slowly gave way to an angry frown.

He glanced at his aunt. "I'll be right back. Don't leave this bed."

With his hand firmly gripping Ivy's arm, he hauled her roughly out of the room. In the hallway, he brandished the letter. "Where the hell did you get this?"

She yanked her arm away and rubbed it gingerly. "Do you enjoy bruising me?" With a glance at the letter, she said, "I picked it up near the stairs. The envelope was opened. Evidently Aunt Tru was reading it on her way upstairs. Why? What's wrong?"

He regarded her suspiciously. "You don't know what's in here?"

She shook her head, and he turned back toward the bedroom.

"Well, aren't you going to let me read it?"

He paused a moment, then turned around to study her questioning look.

"No. If you're telling the truth, I think it's better that you don't know."

"If I'm..." Her voice rose. "You're calling me a liar?"

"Look, Ivy. Stay out of this."

"I'm already in it. I was the one who found your aunt. Remember?"

"Yes. And the one who found this letter." His tone grew ominous. "Very convenient."

She followed on his heels as he stormed into his aunt's bedroom, bewildered by his next words.

"Is this someone's idea of a joke?"

For long moments Gertrude stared at the letter in her nephew's hand. Then she did something completely out of character. She rolled to her side and began to cry.

Stunned, Ivy and Caine could only stare at this un-
believable scene. In all the years they had known this
iron-willed woman, they'd never seen her cry.

With a strangled sound, Ivy snatched the letter from
Caine's hand and read it quickly. A feeling of revul-
sion swept over her.

"Why would someone do this to her?"

Caine was watching her reaction closely. Glancing
at the sobbing woman, he shrugged. "I don't know.
But I intend to get to the bottom of this." He took the
letter from Ivy's hand and folded it before shoving it
in his pocket.

"But why—"

"I said stay out of this, Ivy. It isn't your concern."

She clamped her mouth shut. Dropping to the side
of the bed, she touched the old woman's shoulder and
watched helplessly as she cried out her fears.

The doctor snapped his bag shut and marched down
the stairs to the foyer, where Caine and Ivy were anx-
iously waiting for him.

"Your aunt seems fine." He tried to keep the an-
noyance from his voice. At this moment, she was
probably in better health than his wife, who was no
doubt pacing the floor over their interrupted dinner
plans.

"People don't faint for no reason," Caine said
evenly.

"Your aunt is eighty years old, young man. When
we're her age, we'll probably do a lot of things for no
reason. Now, if you'll excuse me."

The butler helped him on with his coat and handed him his bag. With a brisk handshake, he was gone.

Ivy made her way downstairs to the music room. With a wall of floor-to-ceiling glass panels, it overlooked terraced gardens that Ivy remembered as being a riot of spring color. As she entered, Gertrude and Caine, deep in conversation, looked up. Their talk ceased abruptly.

Embarrassed, Ivy paused in the doorway. "I see I'm early. If you'd like me to wait..."

"No. Come in. Caine was just going to fix us a drink. What would you like?"

She hesitated a moment longer, then took several steps into the room. "Wine. Something dry and red if you have it." She recalled the way Aunt Tru's favorite whiskey had burned. She'd rather not chance it again.

"And I'll have my usual," Gertrude said. Her gaze skimmed Ivy's dress. "I approve. Much better than those awful jeans."

From his vantage point at the bar, Caine studied the slender figure. Her dress of red Chinese silk had a mandarin collar and long, tapered sleeves. The exquisite fabric molded itself to the curves of her softly rounded breasts and hips, then fell in a straight sheath to below her knees. Except for black frog closings, it was unadorned. When she walked, the slits on either side of the skirt revealed an expanse of leg nearly to the thigh.

Ivy had swept her hair back on one side and fastened it with pearl combs. It cascaded over one shoulder in a stream of soft curls.

She glanced up to see Caine studying her and felt a blush warm her skin. Immediately, she looked away.

Caine paused in his work. She had a walk that was just shy of being sinful. Almost too beautiful to be real, she belonged on canvas for the whole world to admire. No model on a magazine cover had ever been as lovely to look at.

He handed his aunt a crystal tumbler of whiskey. Ivy watched the way he moved. So sleek and sure of himself. The dark suit accentuated his dark hair and eyes. Even the perfectly tailored jacket couldn't camouflage the muscles of his arms. When he handed Ivy a tulip glass of wine, their eyes met. If someone spoke, she wasn't aware of it. She knew only that his look was as intimate as a touch. His gaze moved to her mouth and her lips grew warm.

She sipped the wine, cool and dry, and felt her senses sharpen. She needed to walk, talk, do anything to break his hold on her.

She walked to the wall of glass and stared at the freshly turned earth.

"Who does your gardening now, Aunt Tru?"

"We have a lawn and landscape service. They're not nearly as good as your father."

"That's because he loved this place. His work made him so happy."

Gertrude studied her over the rim of her glass. "He did love it here, didn't he?"

Ivy nodded. "When he was injured in that accident and lost his job in the city, it was the low point of his life. But coming back here to his roots was the high point. He said that returning to this land was better than a cure."

Gertrude's tone sharpened. "It's a pity your mother didn't share his opinion of us."

Caine watched Ivy's chin lift defiantly.

"She preferred the city." Ivy looked away and said nothing more in her mother's defense. It was no secret that her mother had resented coming back here. She considered being the wife of a gardener beneath her.

Gertrude sighed. "All the old ways seem to be dying."

Ivy searched her mind for a subject that would cheer the old woman. "Have they planted all the spring flowers you always loved? Tulips, crocus, daffodils?"

Gertrude's voice warmed. "And those little grape hyacinths. How I love them. Yes, they should all be blooming in a few weeks."

Caine walked to the window to stand beside Ivy. "Did you know you're wearing two different earrings?" He smiled and touched an ebony disk from which several strands of jet beads dangled. In her other earlobe was an earring of shimmering opals.

"I couldn't decide which one I liked best. So I wore one of each."

"You're the only woman I've ever met who would do that."

Suddenly self-conscious, she turned away. Her eyes fastened on the painting over the mantel and she let out a little gasp of surprise.

"Aunt Tru. When did you buy that?"

The old woman smiled. "I wondered when you'd notice. Caine told me about it when he saw your exhibit."

Ivy turned wide eyes to him. "You were there? Why didn't you tell me?"

"I was only in New York for a day, then right out again. There was no time."

Ivy walked closer to the fireplace and gazed up at her painting. "It's a scene from the hill behind the house, overlooking the lake. I must have sat and stared at that site a thousand times while I was growing up here. It's one of my favorites."

"Mine too," Aunt Tru said. "When Caine phoned and told me about the painting, I asked him to buy it for me."

"You recognized it?" Ivy asked him.

"I grew up here, too, remember?"

She laughed, and he saw the light that had come into her eyes. If possible, she looked even softer, prettier, when she was laughing.

"Miss St. Martin, your nephew, Darren," Chester announced from the doorway.

"Well, here you all are."

"Darren." The old woman beamed. "I wondered when you'd come down."

"Sorry. I fell asleep. How are you, Aunt Gertrude?" Darren crossed the room and bent to press his lips to her cheek.

"Oh, let me look at you."

Darren St. Martin's hair and skin had been kissed by the California sun. Even his hazel eyes looked golden. His suit bore the unmistakable touch of European tailors and his shirt, tie and Italian leather shoes were impeccable. As usual, he cut a dazzling figure. As he leaned over his aunt, Ivy could see why women were attracted to him—but they were always the wrong kind of women.

Darren turned to Caine. "Hi, big brother. I'm surprised you're here. I thought you were designing an office building or something in Arizona."

Caine smiled and held out his hand. "I was. An office building or something," he mocked. "It's finished now. I'm back home for a while until my next project."

"I can't keep track of all your jobs anymore. I guess there's no rest for the workaholics of this life. You won't find me killing myself with schedules. I've found my niche in life. After watching all those playboys, I've decided that there has to be a better way than living from one paycheck to the other. That reminds me, big brother. I'll have to hit you for a little loan. Just till I get on my feet. Wives are expensive these days. Especially if they're actresses. I think their first lesson is how to find the most expensive stores in town."

Caine lowered his voice. "No problem, Darren. Just let me know how much you need."

"Thanks, big brother. What would I do without you?"

Caine gave a wry laugh. "Probably get a job."

"Or rob a bank."

Darren turned and at that moment caught sight of Ivy standing near the fireplace. "Ivy, is that you?" He rushed to catch her hand. "You look wonderful."

"Hello, Darren. It's been too long."

"It certainly has. I can tell that city life agrees with you. You're looking gorgeous."

As Darren enveloped her in a warm embrace, she smiled up into his face and accepted his kiss. His cologne was an expensive French mixture that she recognized.

"What happened to that drugstore after-shave you used to splash on?" she teased.

"I've outgrown it. I'm a sophisticated man of the world now. I need something that becomes my stature."

"Yuck."

"Yuck? Women don't say things like that to us worldly types."

Caine turned away from them and walked to the bar. He surprised himself by pouring a second drink. Why did the friendly banter between his brother and Ivy bother him? It couldn't be jealousy. He had never been jealous of his younger brother. Protective maybe. Always willing to overlook Darren's lapses. But never jealous. Besides, Ivy Murdock meant nothing to him. So why this twinge? He fought to dismiss the thought. Maybe what really bothered him was the fact that Ivy was so warm and touching with everyone except him. She had practically fallen into Darren's arms. Yet she always seemed to be on guard in Caine's presence. Of course, he could hardly blame her. He'd given her a pretty rough reception. He always seemed a little too grim, a bit too angry in her presence.

Through narrowed eyes he studied Ivy and Darren. They were two of a kind—both beautiful people. He couldn't deny that they made a handsome couple. Darren's blond good looks were the perfect foil for Ivy's dark loveliness.

"Oh, isn't this nice? We're all together again. Just like old times. Darren, come and tell me what you've been doing." Gertrude patted the sofa. "Of course we've read about the separation."

He nodded as he took a seat beside his aunt. "We managed to make the headlines."

"Is it true that Melanie has gone off on that actor's yacht?"

Darren gave a mirthless laugh. "Yes. But it won't last. She'll come back to me. Melanie made it plain that she craves adventure, excitement and lots of money. As soon as I'm solvent, I'll have my little wife back at my side."

Gertrude touched his arm sympathetically. "I know this is a painful time for you, Darren. But when it's resolved, you'll find you've come out of this stronger than ever."

He lifted an eyebrow. "Are you going to give me that old lecture about steel being forged in fire? I'm not steel, Aunt Gertrude. I'm a man. And I've just been burned."

The old woman's voice lowered. "But you'll survive, Darren. And be stronger for it. After all, you're a St. Martin."

He stood and crossed the room, staring down at the flames of the fireplace. "No I'm not, Aunt Gertrude. You're a St. Martin. You act like you've never made a mistake. And Caine." He nodded at his brother.

"Caine's a St. Martin. The two of you are too good to ever make a mistake like mine."

"We've all made them, Darren," Gertrude's voice soothed.

"Have you?" His tone suddenly hardened. "Did your past make you stronger?"

Gertrude froze.

Caine snapped to attention at his brother's sharply issued words.

At the stunned look on his aunt's face, Darren turned away. "And what about old Caine there? Always the perfect example for a younger brother. Maybe I'll take a lesson from him and start living a Spartan existence."

"Darren." Gertrude forced her voice to remain even. "I know you have a right to a certain amount of self-pity. But come over here and talk. We're family. We're always on your side. We want you to work things out."

At her soothing tone, he looked repentant. While he sat beside her, Ivy walked to the bar, where she set down her glass. Then she crossed to the window to look up at the stars that were just becoming visible in the slowly darkening night sky. Caine took her glass, refilled it and stood beside her.

"Thank you."

The scent of her perfume was intoxicating. Caine found himself drawn to her.

For once she was grateful for Caine's silence. She didn't want to make small talk. She wanted to sort out her thoughts. Maybe every family had to struggle through the pain of misunderstanding and bruised egos. Poor Darren. She could feel the pain he was feeling. She wondered if it were possible for a woman like Gertrude St. Martin, a spinster, a woman blessed with both good health and excellent finances, to understand what Darren was going through. And what about Caine? Was he as perfect as Darren painted him?

Despite Darren's problems, she was glad now she had accepted Aunt Tru's invitation. She'd needed to return to her roots again. She'd almost forgotten how peaceful it was here. The fast pace of the city was catching up with her. Maybe that was what had happened to Darren as well. Life in the fast lane could be deadly.

"Penny for them."

She started. "Sorry." She turned to Caine. "I was off in space. I seem to do that a lot."

"Artists can get away with it. People just think you're creating your next masterpiece in your mind." He winked. "Architects, too. When I drift off, my staff thinks I'm designing a monument."

She laughed. "Aren't you ashamed of yourself?"

"Not at all." He grinned. "Once in a while I am designing something. But most of the time I'm just drifting."

She turned to give him her full attention. "You don't look like the sort who drifts. In anything. You're so solid, Caine. I think you could take the whole world's problems and charge through life solving them."

"Thanks for the vote of confidence." His smile faded. "Right now, though, I'd settle for solving just one or two problems."

Ivy glanced at the old woman, her head bent toward the blond one beside her on the sofa. "You don't believe the doctor, do you? It wasn't just a simple fainting spell. It was that terrible letter."

He stared at the amber liquid in his glass, then shrugged. "I don't want to talk about it."

"Did you notice that the letter was mailed in New York City?"

Caine's lips thinned. He remained silent.

"Why won't you talk about it?" she asked.

"Because it has nothing to do with you, Ivy. Unless you wrote it."

She turned away, stung by his words. Every time she thought they were beginning to relax with each other, something happened to remind her to keep her distance. Chester's voice interrupted her thoughts, and the conversation around her stopped as everyone looked up.

"Miss St. Martin, Judge Jacob Tisdale and Mr. David Tisdale."

A young man in a dark business suit stepped past Chester, then paused in the doorway. Beside him, leaning heavily on a cane, stood an old man with white hair and a trim, white mustache.

"Ah. Jacob and David. I wondered what's been keeping you," Gertrude exclaimed, welcoming the newcomers.

The younger man hurried across the room to catch Gertrude's hand. "Miss St. Martin. I'm sorry for the delay. I'm afraid I've been on the phone for hours. Every time I leave my office, they track me down. I've been swamped with work."

The older man followed slowly. With elegant, old-fashioned manners, he bowed slightly and touched Gertrude's hand to his lips before settling down heavily beside her on the sofa.

"I think you know everyone here except Ivy." Gertrude turned. "Ivy, come meet Judge Jacob Tisdale, and his grandson, David Tisdale, my lawyer."

The younger man was lean to the point of being frail. His double-breasted pin-striped suit accentuated his thin frame. His hair was light, but lacked the golden luster of Darren's. With his fair complexion, his blond eyebrows seemed almost nonexistent.

Ivy extended her hand, and stared into pale blue eyes behind wire-rimmed glasses. His smile was pleasant, his handshake firm.

"Hello, David. Though we've never met, I'm familiar with your family name."

"And I've heard of you as well. Our families go back a long way. You probably know my grandfather." He indicated the older man beside Gertrude.

Ivy turned and accepted Jacob's outstretched hand.

The old man studied her carefully, as if searching for some sign of recognition. "William and Diana's daughter?"

She nodded.

"The artist," he said simply.

"And a fine one," Gertrude interjected proudly. "You should have read her reviews, Jacob."

"I did. You showed them to me three times, Gertrude."

Ivy blushed with pleasure and noticed Caine watching her as he poured drinks at the bar. She turned her attention back to Jacob's grandson.

"It's nice that you can work with your grandfather."

"It's been taken for granted that I'd go in the family law firm ever since I was born. I'm the fourth generation to go into law in this county," David said.

His eyes, Ivy noted, didn't look happy.

"And Ivy is the third generation to grow up on the St. Martin estate," Gertrude explained with a smile.

"I know." David seemed mesmerized by her beauty. His pale eyes studied her with keen interest. "Your father had quite a green thumb."

"He was the St. Martin gardener. We lived in the cottage by the gate house."

He nodded. "I know of it. It's been empty for quite a while, hasn't it?"

"Yes. I'm living in New York City now."

"You must find it chaotic after living here."

She saw Caine watching her and smiled. "I've adjusted."

David looked hopeful. "Maybe I could show you around while you're visiting Miss St. Martin."

She avoided Caine's mocking eyes as he handed David a drink. "Thank you. I'd like that."

Ivy was aware that the older man was studying her carefully while she spoke. He seemed intrigued by her. She turned to include him in the conversation. To her discomfort, he continued to stare in silence.

"I'm sorry I was out walking when you arrived, Jacob," Gertrude said, interrupting his thoughts. "I understand you've been in New York City."

He nodded. "Damnable trip. I prefer to stay here as much as I can, but business often dictates otherwise."

"I thought you had finally agreed to retire and allow David to run the business."

He sighed. "More or less. But there are still so many things I've handled for years for my clients, and I feel reluctant to allow young David to take over."

"Including the finances," Gertrude said knowingly.

Ivy smiled at his phrase "young David." Did the old ever allow the young to feel completely in charge?

Gertrude stood, and the older man rose with her. She looped her arm through Jacob Tisdale's. "You look refreshed. Did you sleep?"

He nodded.

"Well, it's time for dinner. You can sit beside me and tell me all about what's been happening in the big city."

With a broad smile, he escorted her to the dining room.

Darren and David Tisdale trailed behind them, carrying on a muted conversation.

Ivy glanced at Caine. "Maybe we should start a romance between your aunt and her counselor. Don't you think they make a lovely couple?"

He gave her a bland look and offered her his arm. "I don't think Trudy is the marrying kind. None of the St. Martins are. But the Tisdales, on the other hand, are very big on marriage."

She stiffened. "What's that supposed to mean?"

"I got the impression that young Tisdale would like to start something with you."

He saw the flash of fire in her eyes. "Don't be silly. We were simply making small talk."

"You didn't see David's heart? It was right there on his sleeve."

"Stop teasing, Caine."

He paused, feeling the touch of silk against his arm. "You've managed to enchant every man in the room, and you claim not to have noticed. Not too sharp, Weed."

He stared down at her, loving the way she blushed when she was angry. "Come on. Let's join the others for dinner."

With a laugh, she tucked her hand in his arm. "You've managed to distract me for the time being. You just said the magic word. Food. I'm famished."

He felt the warmth of her touch and turned his face to inhale the fragrance that lingered even in her hair.

"Good. I like a woman with a healthy appetite."

"Mine's beyond healthy. It's absolutely disgusting."

He gave his best imitation of a leer. "That's even better."

Chapter Three

The dinner had been one of Gertrude's famous seven-course affairs. Long before dessert, Ivy felt uncomfortably full and yearned for a chance to walk off her meal. But her aunt lingered at the table, enjoying her odd assortment of company and their engaging conversation.

Afterward they retired to the library, where Aunt Tru had insisted on two more glasses of her favorite beverage before bidding everyone good-night and leaning heavily on Caine's arm as she made her way upstairs. The others followed.

At a light tap on her door, Ivy opened it to find Chester standing on the threshold.

Caine, emerging from his aunt's room, remained in the shadows, listening.

"You wanted to see me after hours, Miss Ivy?"

She forced herself not to laugh at his stiff demeanor. Chester took his position as butler and head of the household staff very seriously.

"Yes. I wanted to thank you for the help you gave me in that little matter."

"You're welcome. But please don't ever ask me again. It meant invading Miss St. Martin's private quarters. If she knew I'd gone into her personal papers, she'd have my hide."

"I'm sorry, Chester. I hated to make you an accomplice, but I had no choice. Thank you again."

The old man turned away.

Caine waited until he heard Chester's footsteps recede and Ivy's door click shut. His eyes were dark, angry slits. That scatterbrained act was all a cover to hide her real intentions. But why? What did she hope to gain?

Grateful for the night's silence, Ivy slipped off the silk dress and tugged on her old jeans and boots. Shivering in the chill air, she pulled on an oversize sweater. Tucking her hair under a cap, she tossed her leather jacket over her shoulder and made her way quietly down the stairs and out the front door.

A full moon glimmered between layers of slowly drifting clouds. The air was sweet with the fragrance of dogwood and forsythia. The pungent odor of freshly turned earth brought back all those happy memories of her father's years here, taking such delight in his work.

By the light of the moon, Ivy made her way down the long driveway, then veered sharply left to follow the sloping curve of the pond.

Digging her hands into her pockets, she stood by the water's edge and listened to the gentle splash of a frog, startled by her presence. The moon became swallowed up by clouds, leaving her in darkness.

Somewhere to her left, an owl hooted. She heard the snap of a twig and turned, trying to get her bearings. The hair on the back of her neck lifted. Her skin felt suddenly cold, damp. She sensed that she was not alone.

In the blackness of night, a rough hand gripped her arm and spun her around. Before she could react, a hand covered her mouth, stifling her scream.

Her eyes widened. Robbery? Rape? What was happening to her? The pressure remained over her mouth, as she was shoved roughly against the trunk of a tree.

Adrenaline pumped heat through her veins. With all her might, she strained against the arms that held her. She heard a man's grunt as she kicked and thrashed. Her attacker only tightened his grip. She felt strong thighs pressing her against the tree.

Caine's deep voice sent shivers of ice along her spine. "I'll take my hand away if you promise not to scream."

She blinked, nodded.

When he dropped his hand, she took in great gulps of air. Relief flooded through her, leaving her feeling light-headed. Finally catching her breath, she sputtered, "Are you crazy? What's the matter with you?"

At the sound of her voice, he unleashed a stream of curses. "What are you doing out at this time of night?"

"Walking off my dinner."

"In that getup?"

The moon broke free of cloud cover, bathing them in golden light.

She was furious and shaken by his unexpected attack. With venom she sputtered, "What's wrong with my clothes now?"

He stared pointedly at the hat, which left the upper part of her face in shadow. "Nothing's wrong with them. Except that there was no way of telling who you were. You could have been a thief breaking into the estate."

"Oh." She gave a wry smile and peeled off her hat. "There. Is that better?"

Free, her dark hair tumbled wildly about her face and shoulders. At the sight of her, something tightened deep inside him.

"Much better." Without thinking, Caine reached out and caught a silken strand, allowing it to sift through his fingers. His eyes narrowed. It was as soft as he had imagined it would be. Gradually he readjusted his thinking. He should have known the shadowy figure was a woman. He could still feel her softness beneath the bulky clothes. Heat swept through him. "You shouldn't walk alone out here. It isn't safe."

"I've been alone in New York City for seven years now. And I've managed to survive nicely without having anyone hold my hand."

His voice lowered ominously. "I wasn't offering to hold your hand."

His gaze swept her face. If it was possible, she was even lovelier in moonlight. Her hair shimmered, dark and lustrous, touched with red-gold. Her eyes, wide and luminous, gleamed like a cat's in the moon glow. And her lips, full, parted, held the tempting promise of pleasure.

She ran a tongue over lips gone suddenly dry. "I'd better get back." Her sultry voice whispered over his nerves.

Caine knew he should turn away now, before this went any further. Even without touching her more intimately, he thought he knew what her body would feel like pressed to his.

A gentle spring breeze ruffled her hair. He reached a fingertip to it. And just as naturally, his other hand lifted, until without a thought to where it would lead, he plunged his hands into her hair and drew her face to his.

Ivy shivered. Her heart hammered in her chest. It wasn't fear, she knew. It was the nearness of this man. It was the excitement, the anticipation, the expectancy.

She lifted wide eyes to his. His lips brushed hers with a feather-light softness she hadn't expected. Her lids fluttered, then closed, as his mouth covered hers. Excitement surged, hot searing, shocking them both with its intensity.

He had known she would feel like this in his arms. She was soft, melting into him as the kiss deepened.

Her scent, that sweet gentle fragrance of flowers, mingled with the taste of her. He was drowning in her.

His arms came around her to mold her to him. He pulled her closer, closer, until her breasts were crushed to his hard chest. With each shuddering breath, they tormented him. All thought, all his being, were focused on this kiss, on the taste of her.

A loon cried in the night. Caine surfaced and reluctantly lifted his head. Through lowered lids he watched as she struggled for control.

"Caine, I . . ."

"Yes. I know. We'd better go back to the house."

She felt hollow, empty, as if, tasting his lips, she needed more. She wondered if her legs could support her.

His tight voice became a raw whisper, sending a tremor along her spine. "You know this isn't over yet."

"What isn't?" Her eyebrow arched in a question. She laughed. "The weekend or the kiss?"

"Neither. In fact, they've only begun." Without warning he pulled her roughly into his arms and brought his mouth down hard on hers.

Instantly the passion flared. As his mouth moved over hers, his hand roamed her back, drawing her firmly against him.

Stunned, Ivy offered no resistance. Slowly, caught up in the moment, her lips parted and her tongue met his, teasing, touching. She drank in the warm, dark taste of him and felt a little moan rise in her throat. As her hand clutched the front of his jacket, she heard his breath quicken, and felt the thundering of his heart-beat matching hers.

The hands at her back tightened, crushing her against him, until she thought she'd break. Her hands moved along his upper arms, across his shoulders, until they tangled in his thick, dark hair. Still the kiss deepened until all conscious thought fled. There was only this moment, suspended in time, and the feelings that flowed between them. They were alone in the universe. Straining for breath in the midnight blackness, brilliant lights flashed in her brain, blinding her to everything except this man.

"Caine." The word was a strangled cry.

With a supreme effort, Caine pulled himself back from the passion that clouded his mind. He lifted his head and studied her.

Pressing her hands against his chest, she took a step back and tried to calm her rapid breathing.

For long moments neither of them spoke. Finally, when she had composed herself, Ivy whispered, "I'm going back."

"Can you find your way in the dark?"

She met his look. "I found my way here, didn't I?"

He watched as she took a halting step away. Catching her arm, he cautioned, "Watch out for half-hidden rocks. They can trip you up in the darkness."

He felt her tremble as he touched her arm. Instantly he dropped his hand, unwilling to admit the jolt he felt each time he touched her.

"There've been plenty of rocks in my path, Caine. None of them have managed to trip me up." She was already hurrying away, as if eager to escape him.

"There's always a first time." *I'm going to trip you up, lady. Whatever your scheme is, I'm going to be here to catch you.*

This was a first for him. He'd known plenty of women. But he'd never met a woman who had affected him like this. He was still shaken by their kiss.

Leaning against the trunk of a tree, he shook a cigarette from his pack and held a lighter to it. He drew deeply, then exhaled a stream of smoke and stared at the darkened outline of his aunt's mansion.

That kiss had startled him. The simmering passion it unleashed had shocked him with its intensity. Again he inhaled deeply on the cigarette and fought to steady his nerves. Still, he shouldn't have been so surprised. Every time he'd come near her during the day, his pulse rate had gone through the roof.

They were as different as two people could be. Watching her, there were times he swore her feet didn't touch the ground.

All his life, Caine had known only discipline and hard work. He'd always known what he wanted to do, and was willing to do everything necessary to achieve it. The last thing he needed to complicate this already confusing gathering was a gorgeous scatterbrain.

He hadn't expected to kiss Ivy Murdock. He'd come out tonight in search of an intruder. He frowned in the darkness. There was something very wrong about this birthday celebration. Nothing was going as he had planned and there was a real danger lurking in the shadows. He needed his wits about him if he was going to see this business through to its conclusion. He needed a clear mind. Any Ivy was definitely a distraction.

He tossed the cigarette into the pond and started back toward the house. At least, he thought with a wry smile, the days ahead promised to be anything but dull.

As he walked beneath the covered portico and paused at the front door, Caine was surprised to find Ivy still there, frantically searching her pockets.

He let out a low groan. "Oh no. Don't tell me. Let me guess. You forgot the house key."

"It was hanging just inside the door. I hope you brought it."

He frowned, and rummaged through his pockets. Coming up empty, he stood with his hands on his hips. "I can't believe you went out without a key."

"I just didn't think. Besides, stop trying to pass the blame. You did the same thing."

"I had more important things on my mind. Remember?"

"Well," she said with a shrug. "We're locked out. What do we do now—ring the door chimes until someone hears us?"

"We'll have the entire household swarming down here." He paused. "There has to be a way." He thought for a moment, then brightened. "Come on."

Ivy followed him around to the side of the house. Staring up, he said softly, "I've climbed this old trellis dozens of times when I got home later than Aunt Trudy commanded."

"And I thought you were the epitome of honor. Always so noble. The very idea. Sneaking in behind your old aunt's back."

She heard the suppressed anger beneath the sarcastic tone. "I can see that I'm not going to let you in on too many of my past secrets." He tugged on the wooden trellis. "If it hasn't rotted with age, I should be able to get to the balcony."

"And what if the balcony door of your room is locked?"

"I'll force it." He frowned. "It won't be the first time. If you see me disappear inside, walk to the front door. I'll come downstairs and let you in shortly. Unless," he teased, pulling on a strand of her hair, "the climb is too tiring and I decide to go to bed instead of coming to your rescue."

"You wouldn't dare. If you leave me out here, I'll wake the entire state of New York."

Caine didn't doubt it. As he tested the trellis, she called, "And you worried about a thief on the property. Are you sure you aren't a cat burglar in your spare time?"

He placed his foot carefully in a curve of the trellis before beginning the treacherous climb.

Holding her breath, Ivy stared at the darkened outline of Caine's figure as he slowly made his way to the second-story balcony.

Something, some movement above him, caught her eye. Someone was standing on the balcony, watching him. She shifted, straining to make out the figure. It was too dark. Was that an arm raised? Did someone intend to strike Caine before he reached safety?

"Caine. Above you."

He paused in his climb, then lifted his head. The figure darted out of sight.

"Keep your voice down. Do you want to wake the entire household?"

She pressed her lips together. Idiot. He didn't even realize his life might have been in danger.

As Caine disappeared over the railing, she tucked her hair up under her hat and set her foot in the trellis. Feeling around in the darkness above her head for something to hold on to, she began to climb.

Caine had just managed to force open the heavy glass door to his room when Ivy pulled herself over the railing.

"What in the hell . . . ?"

"I needed the exercise," she said, catching her breath from the exertion.

"You know something? You're crazy." He held the door. As she passed in front of him, he inhaled the intoxicating scent of her perfume and felt a familiar tightness deep inside.

"Caine, when I yelled, someone was hovering on the balcony. From where I was standing, it looked like they were going to strike you."

He turned his head to study the darkness. "When I was a boy, I used to see the branches of that old oak outside my window and swear it was someone on the balcony. Are you sure it wasn't just a shadow?"

She bit her lip. At this point, she wasn't sure of anything.

"Come on in, worrywart. And stop trying to make a big mystery out of everything."

She bit back a retort. After all, she'd always had a wild imagination.

Glancing around the luxurious room she whispered, "So this is how the other half lives."

He grinned. "It's humble, but it's home to me."

The king-size bed, which dominated the room, was a brass four-poster, with a headboard reaching nearly to the ceiling. The quilt and pillow covers were of natural hemp and burlap. A sleek contemporary sofa and a pair of art deco chairs surrounded a low brass table. The walk-in closet was bigger than the bedroom of Ivy's New York apartment.

"Umm. Very humble." She walked to a desktop covered with framed photos. There were pictures of a very young Caine in the arms of his mother.

"When did she die?" Ivy asked.

He glanced over her shoulder. "When I was seven. Darren was three weeks old. Three years later, our father married Jenny, Aunt Trudy's younger sister." He pointed to another photo. "That was their wedding picture."

Ivy stared at the young bride and her handsome husband, nearly an exact double for Caine. "Did you like your new stepmother?"

He nodded. "For the short time she was with us. Two years later they were dead in a plane crash. I was twelve, Darren only five. It would have all come crashing down around us if it hadn't been for Aunt Trudy's generosity."

"What do you mean?" She picked up a picture of a solemn little Caine holding a laughing Darren on his lap.

"We had no living relatives so she adopted us. If she hadn't we would have been sent to a state institution. Darren and I probably would have been split up, to be adopted separately."

"How terrible." Ivy set the picture down and studied the photos, almost all of which showed a serious, almost dour little Caine and a laughing, carefree Darren.

Ivy felt a twinge of guilt. She'd always assumed that the St. Martin money made everything easy.

Caine watched her. She was the most beguiling woman he'd ever met, even dressed in that silly cap and leather jacket. He could still recall the softness of her body, the warmth, the fire that blazed at his touch.

Pointing to a picture of the boys in baseball uniforms, she said, "Did you always take everything so seriously?"

He smiled. "I'm afraid so. Darren was one of life's blithe spirits. He was the type who would wander off and get lost the minute my back was turned. He would just touch something and it would break, or end up in his pocket when no one was looking. He loved 'collecting' nice things. I always felt I had to save him from himself."

"Even after you were adopted?" She was unaware of Caine's hand lifting the cap from her head.

His gaze riveted on the mass of dark hair that spilled softly about her face.

"Then I felt even more responsible for him. I realized how much Aunt Trudy was sacrificing to take us in, so I was determined to make it as easy as possible for her." He shook his head, remembering. "With Darren, that was no small task."

Odd, she thought, her first impressions of Caine hadn't been like this at all. She had found him tough, surly, rigid. Now she was seeing another aspect of his personality that she hadn't known existed. The gentle, loving side of a man who cared, really cared about people.

Ivy found herself wondering if Caine's self-imposed task had ever ended, even now. She thought of Darren's carefree life-style, and Caine's dogged determination to succeed.

"How could Aunt Tru adopt you when she wasn't married?"

His hand moved to the collar of her jacket. As he began unbuttoning it, his eyes never left hers. "I'm sure she had to pull a lot of strings. Old Judge Tisdale arranged the adoption when he was still a lawyer."

"With no children of her own, I'm sure Aunt Tru was thrilled to have two boys liven up her house."

He laughed. "That's a nice way of putting it. I think we managed to drive most of the help crazy. Those who didn't quit demanded raises. And got them."

His mouth was just inches from hers. With her jacket open, his hands encircled her waist, measuring her slenderness.

He felt her stiffen as she realized what he had done. She swallowed. His hands slid beneath the sweater to feel her warm flesh.

Her eyes widened. "Don't, Caine." She pressed her hands to his shoulders.

She felt his warm breath feather across her cheek. "Why not? You're here in my room, sharing intimate pictures and memories of my life."

Ivy suddenly felt like an intruder in Caine's life. "I'd better get to bed."

"Not yet." His lips hovered a fraction from hers.

She didn't breathe. She kept her eyes open as he touched his mouth to hers.

He felt the stab of desire, quick, urgent. Lifting his head, he stared down into her eyes. Then slowly, deliberately, his mouth crushed hers. All thought fled. Ivy's hands clutched at his shoulders, drawing him even closer. She felt herself plummeting, dropping from a great height, falling through endless space, locked in those strong arms.

His hands slid along her back, burning a trail of fire along her naked skin.

Dazed, he lifted his head. "You're not wearing anything under this sweater," he muttered against her temple.

"You're very astute, Mr. St. Martin." She tossed her head, trying to think. "I'm leaving. Now."

As she pulled open the door, a figure dashed along the dim hallway, then stopped and turned toward them.

Caine stepped past her. "David. What are you doing?"

The young lawyer hesitated, blinked at the sudden light, then walked toward them. "I heard something, so I got up to investigate." His gaze slid from Caine to Ivy, noting her disheveled appearance. He seemed embarrassed to have caught them together in Caine's room.

"Sorry. I didn't realize what I was interrupting." Before either of them could respond, he hurried away.

With narrowed eyes Caine murmured, "Now I'm responsible for tarnishing your sterling reputation." He touched her cheek, then dropped his hand quickly. "I wish we'd been doing what David assumes. It would have been a lot more fun than climbing walls."

He caught a strand of her hair. At his simple touch, something stirred deep inside her.

His husky voice scraped on her ragged nerves. "In fact, I'll probably be climbing walls all night just thinking about what I've missed."

"Now I know I'm leaving." With a toss of her head, Ivy fled from his touch and began to walk down the hall, then paused and turned. Caine was still standing in the doorway of his room, his dark gaze fastened on her.

"Thanks for an interesting evening. This sure beats the muggers in Central Park."

He inclined his head slightly. "Next time, I'll go to your room, to see your—etchings."

"Funny, Caine. Very funny."

His gray gaze remained on her until she closed her door.

Pulling off his jacket and shirt, Caine opened the balcony door. He held a lighter to a cigarette, then snapped it shut and inhaled deeply. What was happening to him? He was adult, successful, reasonably intelligent. He thought of himself as mildly sophisticated, and there'd been a fair number of women in his life. But this zany, scatterbrained artist, who acted as if she didn't have enough sense to come in out of the rain, was getting to him as no one else ever had. He loved that husky voice of hers, and her joyful laughter. He loved the way her eyes looked, all big and innocent. And a man could get lost in her rich cloud of hair.

He stepped out onto the balcony and watched the clouds scudding across the moon. She was involved in something mysterious. And she had enlisted Chester's aid. That made her the number-one suspect. He intended to watch her closely this weekend.

Ivy was so tired she barely had the energy to undress. Naked, she slipped beneath the covers. But the sleep she longed for eluded her. Instead, thoughts and images crowded her mind.

What was going on in this house? Threatening letters. Mysterious figures on the balcony. The weekend party, which she'd hoped would be a wonderful escape from the pressures of the city, now loomed as a fearsome danger. Ivy opened her eyes in the darkness. She'd always had a wild imagination, even as a very young girl. And always her thoughts were more vivid at night. She would force herself to think of pleasant things.

Caine. She smiled in the darkness. She'd known, almost from the first moment she'd seen Caine today, that he wasn't like anyone she'd ever known before. The attraction was instantaneous. Every time they came near each other, every time they spoke, every time they even looked at each other, sparks flew. That kiss had been as inevitable as breathing.

Yet when they were children, they barely had a chance to know each other. By the time Ivy came to the St. Martin estate, Caine was finishing high school. He went off to college, then to Europe, studying medieval architecture.

Darren, on the other hand, just two years her senior, had been a good friend. They rode the same school bus, studied together after school occasionally and played ice hockey on the duck pond every winter. With so few neighbors in this remote setting, they had accepted each other with good-natured teasing.

How could there be danger or evil in this peaceful rural setting? Ivy punched her pillow and rolled over. If she had to, she would resort to counting sheep to fall asleep. She'd had her fill of thinking.

Chapter Four

It was barely dawn. The first pale pink streak of light began to color the horizon. There was an occasional bird call. Even most of the birds were too sensible to be up yet, Ivy thought, as she walked to the window and drew open the drapes.

She'd slept badly. It wasn't Caine's kiss, she told herself firmly. It was the strange bed. Or maybe it was the sense of unease she'd felt since her arrival. On the surface, everything seemed so normal. But underneath, Ivy sensed that her aunt was caught up in turmoil. There was something unsettling going on here.

Caine was right about one thing. Ivy had never known Aunt Tru to make a fuss about her birthday. Usually she had insisted on ignoring it completely. Why this party? And why this guest list?

She could understand Caine and Darren being invited. After all, they were family. But Ivy hadn't been back here in years. And her mother had made no secret about her unhappiness while she lived here. Why had Gertrude invited Diana Murdock? Judge Jacob Tisdale was obviously an old and dear friend of Gertrude St. Martin. Their friendship spanned half a century, and they seemed comfortable with each other, as only two old friends can be. There was a special softness in the old man's eyes when he looked at Gertrude. Almost, Ivy thought, like a look of love. His grandson, David, was nice enough, although at times he seemed out of his element. He and Darren had spent some time talking together, and Ivy had gathered that they were talking business. That made sense. If David's law firm represented Gertrude, he would be the obvious choice to counsel her nephews as well.

After a quick shower, Ivy pulled on her jeans and oversize sweater and headed for the kitchen. She hoped the staff wasn't up yet. She disliked life in general and people in particular, until she had had several cups of morning coffee.

In the doorway of the kitchen, she stopped. Caine had apparently had the same idea. With the fragrance of freshly roasted coffee heavy in the air, he looked up from the paper he was reading to give her a quick glance.

"If you want anything more than coffee, you have to fix it yourself. Martha refuses to start her day before seven."

"Suits me. Just coffee. And please, no conversation."

"Right."

He held out his cup as she passed. She took it to the counter and filled it, then filled a cup for herself.

"How do you take it?"

"Hot and black."

"Good." That saved her searching for cream or sugar. "Me too." She placed his cup beside him.

Caine handed her a section of the morning newspaper he'd been reading. Without a word, she sat across from him and read her paper, savoring the excellent coffee and the silence. The only sounds were the chirping of birds and the rustling of the newspaper.

Nearly an hour passed before either of them bothered to speak. But each time she turned a page of the paper, she darted quick glances at the solemn figure across the table.

"More coffee?"

She shook her head. "No. I've finally had enough. I think I'll make it through another day."

"Made any plans?"

She nodded. "I think I'd like to visit the cottage. And later on, if the sun is shining, I'd like to take a walk and try a few sketches."

"I was planning to see the cottage, too. Mind if I tag along?"

"No. As long as you don't mind riding on the back of my bike."

Caine looked skeptical. "Depends. How good a driver are you?"

"Depends." She laughed. "How good a passenger are you?"

"I guess I have no choice. I'll be the perfect gentle-man."

They both looked up at the sound of Chester and Martha discussing the day's work schedule in the other room.

"Time to duck out. The troops are arriving."

Catching her hand, Caine led Ivy out the back door. Chuckling like two conspirators, they hurried to the garage.

As he pulled open the heavy door, she gunned the engine of the motorcycle.

"Hop on."

It seemed incongruous that the slender, almost fragile woman he had held in his arms last night could actually transport them both safely on that gleaming machine. He gave her a dubious look.

"Come on. Stop being such a coward."

"I'm only a coward when I'm asked to put my life in the hands of a woman who looks like she wouldn't know the difference between a piston and a spark plug."

She cut the engine. The silence was shocking.

"A piston is a sliding piece moved by or moving against fluid pressure, which usually consists of a short cylinder fitting within a cylindrical vessel along which it moves back and forth. A spark plug, on the other hand, is a part that fits into the cylinder head of an internal-combustion engine and carries two electrodes separated by an air gap across which the current from the ignition system discharges to form the spark for combustion."

Caine's mouth dropped open.

With a smug look, Ivy started the engine once more. Over the din she shouted, "Care to ride with poor, dumb, little old me? Or would you rather walk?"

Caine threw back his head and roared with laughter. Then with a shake of his head, he climbed on behind her and wrapped his hands around her waist.

For a moment, the touch of his hands was so shocking, she felt paralyzed. Then, forcing herself into action, she gunned the engine and they sped along the driveway.

The wind created by the motion of the vehicle was invigorating. The floral scent of her cologne enveloped them. Pressing himself firmly against her back, Caine brought his lips to her ear. She felt a delicious tingle and increased their speed.

His hands tightened beneath her rib cage. "Umm. This is the only way to fly."

She laughed, and the sound was carried away on the wind. Her hair fanned out in the breeze, and he buried his face in a tangle of curls, loving the feeling of being lost in a cloud of burnished silk.

Without slowing down, the motorcycle took the curves in the driveway and careered around a sharp bend. When Ivy moved, Caine moved with her. Their bodies were in such perfect harmony, their every move looked choreographed. They leaned and straightened like a single figure.

When they pulled up to the deserted cottage and Ivy cut the engine, they both experienced a letdown after the exhilaration of the ride.

"Damn." He seemed genuinely surprised. "You're good."

She warmed to his compliment.

Caine climbed off the bike and stood back to admire the view of her sleek form as Ivy swung her long leg over the vehicle. When it was parked, he took her hand and led her to the door. He pulled a key from his pocket, then was puzzled when the door swung open before he could insert the key in the lock.

"Aunt Trudy said she kept it locked."

Ivy shrugged and followed him inside. "Maybe the lock is old and rusted."

Caine checked the lock, then the key. Wordlessly he pocketed the key.

Stripped of their furnishings, the rooms seemed so much larger than Ivy remembered. It was a simple, one-story floor plan. There was a combination living-dining room with a large fieldstone fireplace, a cozy kitchen, two bedrooms, each with its own bath, and a combined laundry and workroom.

Ivy could still picture her father, his sleeves rolled above his elbows, potting a precious plant from the garden. The house always smelled of rich, dark soil and the fragrance of dozens of herbs and flowers.

Silently, almost reverently, Ivy moved from room to room, allowing happy memories to wash over her. In the kitchen, the rays of the rising sun streamed through the dirty windows and reflected little rainbow prisms on the white stucco walls.

"We always had the morning sun in here." She spoke softly, as if afraid to speak aloud. "It was a wonderful way to start the day."

To Caine's experienced eye, the sturdy beams, the wonderful antique leaded windows, the excellent craftsmanship were all good reasons for renovating the old place.

"It's a shame to see it lying vacant," Ivy muttered.

"Would you like to see it lived in again?"

She looked up. "Of course."

"I've been thinking about remodeling it for a weekend retreat."

A smile lit her eyes before she spoke. "It would be a wonderful place to come to. The kitchen would need to be modernized. But the plumbing is in good shape." She shrugged. "I'm not so sure about the old furnace. But the fireplace throws enough heat to warm all the rooms." She wistfully continued, "I used to love to snuggle up by the fire and read on long winter nights."

With Caine following her, she hurried to the living room. "Dad said these stones all came from St. Martin property. They were hauled here and fitted, stone by stone, into this fireplace."

As she spoke, she bent to pick up a chunk of stone that lay on the hearth. "That's odd. One side of this looks like it's been cut out."

Caine took it from her and examined it. Studying the stones along the fireplace, he held it up to a gaping hole between two other stones. It fit perfectly.

"It has been cut." As Caine lifted the stone to set it into the opening, he noticed the dull gleam of metal deeply recessed in the fireplace. "There's something back here." He stood on the hearth and peered into the opening. "This stone hid a small metal safe." His eyes narrowed. "Did you know that it was there?"

Ivy shook her head and climbed up beside him. Standing on tiptoe, she stared at the spot he indicated. "I've never seen it before."

Caine forced himself to ignore the delicate scent of her perfume. Fighting the hypnotic spell, he studied her eyes. His heart contracted. Like him, she had risen early. Had she been aware of a hidden safe in the cottage? Did it contain something she didn't want anyone else to know about? Had she intended to get to the cottage before anyone else? Just how good an actress was she? Was he really in the company of an innocent, or did she know more than she was willing to admit?

"Want me to open it?"

Her eyes widened. She swallowed, then nodded her head. He pulled the small metal door open. The safe was empty.

"Someone knew about it."

"How could they? This was my home for ten years, and I never knew about the safe."

"This cottage was built at the same time as all the other buildings on the St. Martin estate. The safe could have been included in the original construction plans. That means that plenty of other people could have known about this safe."

"Has anyone lived here since I moved out?"

"No. Aunt Trudy said the cottage has been vacant."

He glanced around. Until now, he hadn't bothered to notice the footprints at the entranceway, or the muddied imprint of a flat shoe—a man's shoe—or a woman's boot. From the looks of it, there had been a steady stream of visitors to this little cottage.

He shrugged. "The cottage has been vacant a long time. Anyone could take as much time as they wanted to search the place."

"But what do you think my father kept in that safe?"

Caine frowned. "I wish I knew."

Ivy shivered. Caine drew her close and wrapped his arm around her shoulder, wondering if he was a fool to try to convince himself of her innocence.

"I don't want to stay here, Caine."

He read the fear in her eyes. "Relax. This could have been done a year ago or more."

"Or yesterday. That cut on the stone looks fresh."

He had thought the same thing. She was suddenly displaying more sense than he would have credited her with yesterday. He couldn't figure her out. Was she a scatterbrain or was that just a clever cover?

"I want to leave, Caine." He felt the tremor that ran through her as his hand caressed her shoulder.

"I just want to look a little longer."

"Fine. I'll wait for you outside."

The thought of strangers going through her home, desecrating her memories, disturbed her more than she cared to admit. Why had her father never told her about the safe? And what had he kept there? Did her mother know? Ivy's hands clenched at her sides. Even if Diana knew, she wouldn't have shared that knowledge with Ivy. Mother and daughter had shared so little. Ivy felt the sudden, unexpected sting of tears. She had been such a disappointment to her mother.

Caine spent another half hour going through the cottage. While one part of his mind searched for some meaning to this additional piece of the mystery, the other part of his mind automatically began designing the changes he would make in these rooms.

Caine's taste ran to sleek, contemporary lines, both in architecture and furnishings. He'd always been attracted to clean, sophisticated beauty. But something about the cottage prompted him to alter his thinking. As he walked through the cozy rooms, pausing to study the small, leaded windows, and standing back to admire the wood beams and paneled walls, he began to visualize plump, upholstered sofas, an antique writing desk, a cluster of potted plants.

This cottage wasn't a typical bachelor's refuge. It was a lovers' retreat. It almost begged for two people to share its warmth and intimacy.

Caine's thoughts turned to the mysterious woman who waited for him outside. Ivy was an enigma. A contemporary woman, she was living on her own in New York, making a name for herself in the art world. Her odd taste in fashion, and the fact that she insisted on driving that ridiculous motorcycle, proved that she was strong enough to defy convention. Yet there was something so old-fashioned about her. Maybe it was her quirky sense of humor, or her fierce loyalty to an old woman three times her age. Whatever it was, Ivy Murdock was a puzzle. And he was spending entirely too much time thinking about her.

When he emerged, Ivy was standing with her back to him, her arms hugged tightly to herself, her face turned up to the sun. He paused to enjoy the way the sunlight turned the ends of her hair blue-black. As he studied her slim figure he felt the familar tightening deep inside him.

Walking up behind her, he murmured her name.

She turned. Her features relaxed into a smile and his gaze fastened on her mouth. What happened next stunned them both.

He held out a hand. Before she could take it, he reached out and caught a strand of hair and wound it around his finger, drawing her head up.

Puzzled by the look on his face, she arched an eyebrow. He touched a finger to her cheek, and reveled in the softness of her skin. Following the curve of her cheek, he traced the fullness of her lips, feeling their velvet wetness. Impulsively, he dipped his finger inside her lower lip. At the pleasant sensations, her mouth opened. She gasped. He could read the surprise in her eyes.

He cupped her face in his hands and lowered his lips to hers. He hadn't intended for this to happen. But he had to kiss her again, to see if what had passed between them last night was real, or only a fantasy brought on by the moonlight.

"No, Caine."

His gray eyes seemed opaque in the sunlight.

"Why don't you stop me?"

His lips covered hers.

He had expected warmth, tenderness, some pleasant sensations. He'd even hoped to revive the simmering passion he had felt in her. What he hadn't anticipated was the hard, driving need that rocketed through him the moment he took her lips. His hands thrust deeply into her hair, holding her head when she would have pulled away. A white hot light seemed to sear his brain, blinding him to everything except his need for her.

Frantically her hands pushed against his chest. As he took the kiss deeper, he felt her hands relax, then curl into his shirt, pulling him closer.

She smelled of soap and spring flowers. Clean. Fresh. Her breath was sweet, mingling with his. For a moment the kiss softened, as he pulled her into the circle of his arms. She sighed, and wrapped her arms around his waist.

She could feel his thighs pressing against hers. Her breasts were crushed to his chest. A heartbeat hammered. Hers or his. Or both. As he drew her even closer, she could feel his hard body imprinting itself on her softness.

She'd never known a surge of passion like this. The heat of his body, his caressing fingertips, his seductive mouth, were taking her higher than she'd ever been.

With a little sob, she called his name. Or thought she did.

He lifted his head. Through narrowed eyes he studied her. Her eyes were so wide, they looked too big for her face. Her lips were moist and parted, swollen from his kisses. Her hair, tangled by his rough hands, drifted about her face.

He knew he should pull away now. But the need for her was too great. With a sigh of resignation he drew her once more into his arms. He kissed the corners of

her eyes, her cheeks, her earlobes, then brought his
mouth to her throat.

"Ivy. Little weed." He murmured her name against
her skin as his mouth explored her throat, the hollow
of her shoulder, her collarbone.

The need grew, catching them by surprise, until it
became pain.

He caught at her lower lip with his teeth, then covered her mouth with his. His hands at her hips drew
her firmly to him, tormenting both of them. Her
hands sought his skin, and she felt his sudden intake
of breath as she slipped her hands beneath his shirt.
Passion became a kind of madness, taking over their
control. Between their tightly pressed bodies, his
hands sought her breasts. His thumbs stroked. She
drew him closer.

The spring sunshine bathed them in its golden rays.
The air was sweet with new flowers, but it was Ivy's
scent that filled Caine's mind. The softness of her
body, the taste of her skin, the texture of her hair.
There was nothing but this woman, and the need, the
raw, driving need.

Caine knew he had to stop this torment. For one last
minute, he savored the taste of her lips, the feel of her
skin. Then he forced himself to step away.

They were both too shaken to speak. Dragging in
deep breaths of air, Ivy willed herself to stand very
still. She was afraid that at any moment her legs would
refuse to hold her.

"You shouldn't have done that."

He clutched his hands at his side, forcing himself not to touch a finger to her swollen lips. "I had to. And I'll probably have to again."

They heard the footsteps a moment before the voice.

"Well, I thought I was the only one out exploring this early in the morning." David Tisdale's words were a dash of ice water.

Two heads snapped to one side. Ivy and Caine started guiltily, then blinked at the figure of the young lawyer. How long had he been there? How much had he seen?

"What are you doing here?" Caine's voice was hard.

"Just out walking. I asked Darren to meet me here at the cottage." David's neck bore the flush of recognition. He studiously avoided their eyes. Glancing at his watch, he said, "He should be here anytime now. And you?"

Caine waited, fighting for composure. "Just looking around."

Caine watched the way Ivy's hair lifted on the breeze. He tried to keep his voice casual as he said to her, "Why don't you go back to the house? I think I'll stay here awhile and walk around the property. It'll give me a better perspective for the remodeling job."

She nodded, not trusting her voice. Her legs were wooden as she walked to the bike. As she climbed on the motorcycle, she prayed it would start on the first attempt. She needed to get away from probing eyes. The ride would clear her head.

As she started the engine, Caine shook a cigarette from the pack and held it between his lips. He didn't bother lighting it in front of David. The wind was too strong to allow the match to burn. Besides, he was afraid his hand was none too steady.

Chapter Five

Small clouds dotted a blue sky. Warm spring sunshine spread liquid gold over fields washed clean of winter's grime. The view was a pastoral scene of rolling hills and thick wooded forests. Though pockets of snow still clung stubbornly in shadowed areas and at the base of trees, a fine lacy veil of pale green buds adorned the trees, proclaiming the advent of spring.

Ivy sat in a clump of new grass. Clad in the ever-present jeans and a shirt tied at her midriff, she studied the landscape, then bent over the tablet, sketching.

The sun was warm on her back. As she worked, her hair fell across one shoulder and spilled over her breast. Lifting her head, she studied the scene, then traced quick patterns on the paper.

How could she have imagined someone on the balcony last night? Why had she allowed her imagination to run wild? Threatening letters. Blackmail. Here? She allowed her gaze to travel over the gently rolling landscape. This was hardly a setting that spoke of dark, mysterious deeds.

It was that childhood curse. Clouds became castles. Molehills became mountains. Shadows became enemies.

Flipping the page, Ivy immersed herself in her work. That was the only cure for it. Once she lost herself in her art, she could blot out all thought.

Caine stood in the shadow of a gnarled oak and watched the slender figure below him. Sitting cross-legged on the side of the hill, she looked like a child with a coloring book. The breeze caught little wisps of hair, lifting them from her neck. The sun sought out all the colors of her hair, from lush ermine to rich inky black.

Shaking a cigarette from the pack, he held a lighter to the tip, then inhaled deeply. Through narrowed eyes he blew out a stream of smoke and leaned a hip against the trunk of the tree.

Not a child; a woman. Tomboy and temptress. She was the most surprising woman he'd ever met. She didn't even seem aware of her beauty. That was part of her charm.

He watched as her hands moved deftly, sketching a stand of evergreens on a distant hill. She was so immersed in her work, she was unaware of his presence. Now he could take his time and watch her without her knowledge.

He studied the pale skin exposed at her midriff. It was the sort of skin that wouldn't darken even in the sun. There was a translucent quality to it, revealing the fine blue veins just below the surface. He longed to touch it.

She shifted her position, stretching out long legs and leaning on one elbow as she continued to sketch. The movement sent her hair drifting softy about her face in a thick, lush cloud. What he wouldn't give to see that hair rippling against the cool, white pillow on his bed. The thought startled him. A slow smile softened his harsh features. Yes, to touch her pale skin, to watch her eyes darken and grow heavy-lidded at his touch. To feel again the excitement, the hard, driving need that he had experienced when he had taken her in his arms.

At the call of a bird, she looked up and watched its slow, circling flight. Turning, she caught sight of Caine behind her.

"You startled me. How long have you been here?"

He stubbed out the cigarette and walked closer. "Just a few minutes." Glancing down at the sketch on her tablet, he added, "Can't keep away from it, I see."

He saw the smile touch her eyes. "No. What about you? Do you find yourself always studying the architecture in every town you visit?"

"Of course. It's as much a part of me as eating and sleeping."

Her eyes softened. "Yes. You would understand." She chuckled. "So few people really do, you know. They don't realize that we're constantly recording everything for use later. I study the way the horizon looks early in the morning, with little ribbons of color just beginning to light the dawn. I memorize the way a mountain peak rises out of the hills, reaching majestically to the sky. Do you do that with buildings?''

He nodded. ''I used to stand on this hill when I was a boy and love the way Aunt Trudy's house blended in with the woods. The builder used only native materials. The stone, the wood, look as if they belong here.''

Excited at finding a kindred spirit in Caine, Ivy confided, ''In New York, I close my eyes and can see so much of this place. But I've discovered that I didn't recall the little things. Like that hill over there.'' She pointed. ''I'd forgotten how the trees grow in little clusters here and there, with large open spaces between.''

''For crops,'' Caine said, dropping down beside her. ''The farmers cleared much of the woods for planting crops. But they left enough of the trees to keep the hills from eroding.''

Her face changed expression at this new understanding. ''I never thought about that before. Yes,'' she said nodding. ''It makes sense.''

''Anything else you'd like to know,'' he offered, leaning back on his elbows, ''just ask.''

Adopting his mock-serious attitude, she leaned back beside him. Their shoulders brushed, sending a tingling sensation along her spine. She glanced at Caine, then quickly looked away.

''I've always wanted to meet a walking encyclopedia. As a matter of fact, there are a few things I'd like to know.''

He turned and met the green gaze. "Such as?"

"Does Darren always turn to you when things go wrong in his life?"

Caine plucked a blade of grass and slid it between his teeth. Lost in thought, he was silent for long moments before responding.

"I've come to expect it. And I suppose he has, too. He was just a baby when we lost our parents. I felt responsible for him. I think I always will."

"But isn't that unhealthy? Doesn't it encourage Darren to lean too heavily on you?"

Caine's tone held the edge of sharpness. "He's no burden."

"I didn't suggest that he was. But maybe one day Darren will resent the fact that he can't take all the credit for his own success. Don't you see, Caine? If you pick him up each time he stumbles, he won't feel that he's made it on his own."

Caine grew thoughtful. "I never thought about it. I suppose you're right. But as long as he asks for my help, I'll be there to give it to him. There's no way I could ever refuse Darren."

Yes. She had seen the way he responded to his younger brother's every need.

"How did you feel about changing your name to St. Martin when Aunt Tru adopted you and Darren?"

The question surprised him. Ivy could see the cloud of pain the memories evoked.

He thought a moment before answering. "It was harder for me. I was twelve. But I was so worried about what would happen to us without the adoption, I agreed immediately. Darren was only five. I knew that within a few years, he would completely forget his real name." Caine glanced at the wispy leaves of a young sapling. "There were some twinges of guilt. I felt that I had somehow betrayed my father by giving up his name. But as I grew to love Gertrude, I realized how much it meant to her to have heirs. She often told us that before we came along, she had resigned herself to the fact that when she died, the St. Martin line would be ended. And with it, the St. Martin name."

"I wonder why she never married."

"She rarely talks about her youth. I gather, from little things she said, that she wasn't close to her father. In fact, I think their relationship was very stormy. She's had to be a strong, gutsy woman."

"You love her a lot, don't you?"

He nodded.

"Why would anyone want to hurt her?" The words tumbled out before she had time to think.

Immediately Caine's smile faded. His features became stiff and tense. "Stay out of it, Ivy."

"But I just can't understand how someone could hurt an old woman."

"Do you think the whole world is made up of good, generous souls?" Caine stood, towering over her. His gray eyes darkened with anger. "There's evil in this world. Most of us are capable of it. It's pervasive. It even finds its way into sleepy little towns, and secluded estates. There are a lot of selfish people out there who don't give a damn about anyone but themselves."

She stood and clutched her sketch pad to her chest. "Why don't you call the police?"

"Because there's been no threat made, and no actual demand for money."

"Are you worried about her safety?"

His face seemed impassive. "I'll see to her safety."

"Do you know how many people will be here tonight for the party?"

Caine shook his head. "I've asked Aunt Trudy for the guest list. There are too many people invited to keep an eye on everybody. But I intend to stick close to her."

"What about the servants?"

Caine placed a hand beneath her elbow as they climbed the hill and followed a path back to the house. Instantly he felt the jolt. There was no cure for it. Each time he came near her, he wanted her.

He fought to keep his thoughts on other matters. "Most of them have worked for Aunt Trudy for years. She trusts them."

"And you?"

"I don't trust anyone."

"Even me?"

He didn't respond.

She looked away. "Have there been other threats?"

Caine paused. Why did he want to share his thoughts with Ivy? He had always been an intensely private person. But something about this woman made him instinctively want to talk to her. Despite his suspicions, he could read truth in her eyes. And honor.

His voice deepened with emotion. "There was one other letter."

"What did it say?"

He regarded her in silence, then turned and began walking beside her. "It mentioned a secret in her past that she has never revealed."

Now it was Ivy's turn to stop. "Aunt Tru? I don't believe it."

"She's lived a long and full life, Ivy. In almost everyone's life there are things they would rather not have revealed. She's only human, after all. But that doesn't give anyone the right to dredge up the past. If there's something that she's ashamed of, it's her business. She deserves her privacy."

"But you think there's some connection to whatever was taken from my parents' safe, don't you?"

He stared down at her. "It could be."

As they rounded a corner of the house, Ivy saw the low-slung, red sports car in the driveway. Caine saw her stiffen.

At the door, Chester announced, "Miss Ivy. Your mother is here. I've given her a room in the south wing. She's waiting for you upstairs in the sitting room with Miss St. Martin."

She forced a stiff smile. "Thanks, Chester."

Caine trailed behind as she walked slowly up the stairs. He remembered the way she had bounded up these very stairs when she arrived, all breathless and hopeful.

In the doorway of the sitting room, he saw her take a deep breath and square her shoulders.

"Hello, Mother."

Diana Murdock turned at the sound of her daughter's distinct, low voice.

"I see some things never change." She stared pointedly at the sketchbook in Ivy's hand. Her gaze skimmed the figure in faded jeans, then paused a moment at the blouse tied at her midriff. "Gertrude has been trying to convince me that you're earning some respect in your little art world. I'll believe it when I see it. Couldn't you at least dress the part of a successful woman? And that hair. Ivy, I think it's time to dispense with the Alice-in-Wonderland look for something a bit more sophisticated."

To Gertrude, Diana added, "Lord knows I've tried. I've offered to take her shopping and to my hairdresser. But Ivy has always had a rebellious streak in her nature."

Ignoring the taunt, Ivy brushed her lips across the cool cheek. "How nice that you could make it for Aunt Tru's birthday party. Doesn't she look well?"

Watching her, Caine wasn't fooled by Ivy's cool demeanor. Her churning emotions were evident in her eyes.

"Yes. Did I forget to mention it, Gertrude? You're looking very well."

Ignoring the tepid compliment, the old woman lifted a hand. "Diana, you remember my nephew, Caine, don't you?"

Dark eyes appraised him, noting the faded denims and nondescript sweater. If it hadn't been for his rugged handsomeness and cool, gray eyes, she would have dismissed him. But it was impossible to easily dismiss a man like Caine. There was about him an aura of quiet strength, and something even more compelling—power.

She smiled and extended a beautifully manicured hand to him. "Hello, Caine. It's been years."

"Diana."

Diana Murdock was small, standing barely five feet three inches. Her figure was as trim as a schoolgirl's. She wore her hair short and very blond. Her suit was a pale orchid knit. Her lipstick, eye shadow and nail polish were a perfectly matched shade of orchid.

Her passion had always been clothes. Although her husband had left her a sizable insurance fund, she was forced to live a modest existence. Her New York apartment was small, her life-style simple. But her clothes, like the woman and her tastes, were elegant.

"Do you live here with your aunt?" she asked Caine.

"No."

When he volunteered nothing further, Gertrude added, "Caine lives in New York City, when he isn't flying off around the country. But I've persuaded him to renovate your old cottage, so he can spend an occasional weekend here."

"I don't understand why you'd want to sink any money into that little place." Diana's lips pursed.

"I spent some time there this morning. I thought it was charming." Caine winked at Ivy as he crossed the room to sit beside his aunt.

"Remind me to ask you sometime for your definition of charming." Diana sniffed.

Caine glanced at his aunt. "By the way, Trudy, I thought you kept the cottage locked."

"I do. Why?"

"The door was unlocked this morning. I didn't need the key you gave me."

"I don't understand. I've ordered Chester to check the buildings on the estate every week. I'm sure no one has visited the cottage since..." She looked up. "That reminds me, Diana. Did you find whatever it was you were looking for in the cottage?"

"Yes." Diana picked up the cup of tea at her elbow, avoiding Gertrude's eyes.

"What were you looking for, Mother?"

"Some books of your father's. I drove up a few weeks ago and asked Gertrude's permission to go through the attic for whatever we had left behind."

Ivy felt a tightening around her heart.

"Will you two have tea, or would you rather join me in something stronger?"

"Nothing for me," Ivy said, standing quickly and hurrying to the door. "I think I'd like to bathe and rest before the party."

"Remember. Cocktails in the music room at six."

"I'll remember." Ivy's gaze shifted from her mother to Caine. He had to know what she was thinking. He was too sharp to have missed what her mother said.

"And Ivy," her mother said coldly, "wear something appropriate. I don't want to be embarrassed at the gathering this evening."

"You needn't worry, Mother. The last thing I want to do is embarrass you."

She turned away, missing the scowl that darkened Caine's face. Even the usually placid Gertrude frowned at the tension she could feel between mother and daughter.

"If you'll excuse me, I have some things to take care of." Caine stood and followed Ivy from the room, leaving his aunt and Diana alone to fill the uncomfortable silence.

As she climbed the stairs, Caine caught Ivy by the arm. "Ivy."

He felt her stiffen. "Let me go, Caine."

"I saw how you reacted. Are you suggesting you suspect your own mother now?"

A tremor shuddered through her slender frame. "Don't you?"

He could sense her suffering. "The cottage has been vacant a long time. There was plenty of time for anyone to break in and search it. You saw how many footprints marred the entrance."

Her voice lowered to a whisper. "That cottage was completely empty when we left. My father kept no books in the attic. There were only old snapshots of him as a boy. My mother left them behind when she moved."

"Maybe she decided she wanted them after all."

"I doubt that."

His mind raced. Trying to change the subject, he casually said, "Your mother seems awfully young."

Ivy kept her back to him. "She was only eighteen when they were married. Dad was thirty-six." In her compassion, Ivy began to defend her mother, as she had always defended her to others. "It must have been difficult for her, being a child and trying to raise one." He heard the slight break in her voice. "As you can tell, I've never lived up to her expectations."

Caine caught her by the shoulders and turned her to face him. "Is that a frown?" He ran a finger along the furrow that creased her brow.

"My father always called it an upside-down smile."

"Then I'll just turn you on your head to make you look happy." Caine kept his hand on her arm, while he stared down into her upturned face. "You were very close to your father, weren't you?"

He watched the frown disappear. "Yes. He was special. Maybe because he waited so long to marry and have a child. He always knew how to make me laugh. When I grew taller than my mother, taller than any of my classmates and felt awkward and ugly, my father always made me feel beautiful, even though I knew he was only trying to lift my spirits."

"My God, Ivy, you don't know, do you?" Caine traced a finger along her cheek.

He saw the puzzled look in her eyes. "Know what?"

He bent and brushed his lips across her forehead. "Your father wasn't just trying to make you feel better about yourself. You really are beautiful. Believe me. All the men at the party tonight will have a special treat just watching you."

She turned away, feeling the heat stain her cheeks. "Don't tease, Caine."

She was pulled roughly into his arms. His voice was gruff. "I've always been attracted to beautiful things. Don't you understand that when I look at you I see a beautiful, desirable woman?"

She felt her pulse leap. Staring into his eyes, she saw herself reflected there. She ran her tongue over her lips, and saw his gaze focus on her mouth.

First
Class
Romance

Delivered to your door by

Silhouette Romance®

(See inside for special 4 FREE book offer)

Find romance at your door with 4 FREE novels from Silhouette Romance!

Slip away to a world that's as far away as your mailbox. A world of romance, where the pace of life is as gentle as a kiss, and as fast as the pounding of a lover's heartbeat. Wrap yourself in the special pleasure of having Silhouette Romance novels arrive at your home.

By filling out and mailing the attached postage-paid order card you'll receive—FREE—4 new Silhouette Romance novels (a $7.80 value) plus a FREE Mystery Gift.

You'll also receive an extra bonus: our monthly Silhouette Books Newsletter. Then approximately every 4 weeks we'll send you six more Silhouette Romance novels to examine FREE for 15 days. If you decide to keep them, you'll pay just $11.70, with no extra charge for home delivery and at no risk! You'll have the option to cancel at any time. Just drop us a note. Your first 4 books and Mystery Gift are yours to keep in any case.

Silhouette Romance®

"I have to get ready."

His voice was a low growl. "Go ahead and run away, Ivy. There'll be another time." As she started to pull away, he murmured against her ear, "You can count on it."

Chapter Six

Ivy leaned back in the tub, allowing the warm water to soothe her taut nerves. Her mother's cool reception reminded her once again how distant they had become. Did all families experience such troubles, she wondered. Or was her family a special case?

She thought of Gertrude St. Martin, a lonely spinster yearning for children of her own, and willing to adopt two little boys who didn't have a family. It was sad that she never married and experienced the joy of her own children. Thank heavens for Darren and Caine.

Caine displayed more nurturing, more capacity to love than her own mother. He was a man who would always be counted on to help a younger, less disciplined brother. And his concern for Gertrude was genuine.

Draping a bath sheet around herself, she stepped from the tub and began brushing her hair. She ought to be grateful to her mother. It was probably Diana's constant disapproval that had taught Ivy such early independence. She had always known she would have to stand alone one day. The loneliness of her New York apartment was nothing compared with the loneliness she had suffered at the hands of her mother after her father's long illness and death.

Ivy slid her long legs into sheer panty hose, then pulled on a brief, silk teddy of palest green, the color of sea foam. This was one of her few extravagances. She loved the whisper of silk against her skin. Carefully applying makeup, she added a blush of color to her cheeks, and a hint of pale green to her eyelids. From the closet she removed a cocktail-length gown of emerald-green silk and slipped it over her head. She'd found this dress in the Village, in the shop of a friend who collected antiques, and had fallen in love with it. The sleeves were full to the elbow, then tapered to long, narrow cuffs with a dozen buttons to the wrist. The neckline was draped in front and dipped very low in back. The fabric molded to the soft curves of her body, then fell in gentle folds about her calves. She slipped her feet into matching strappy sandals, then brushed her hair loose and caught it behind one ear with a tortoiseshell comb. She wore no jewelry, except tiny pearl earrings. Adding a touch of gloss to her lips, she twirled for a final inspection.

What would Caine see when he looked at her? She dismissed the thought instantly, annoyed that it had crept unbidden into her mind. She had learned to live her life never caring what others thought. What mattered was how she felt about herself. Each day she grew stronger, more content within herself. The brief encounter with her mother had painfully brought back all their differences, all the old insecurities. But it was too late for Diana to destroy Ivy's self-confidence now. She might slip and stumble, but she wouldn't fall.

She forced herself to think of happier things. Tonight was Aunt Tru's birthday party. A time of joy and celebration. At least for tonight, she felt beautiful.

Taking a small, wrapped package from the drawer, Ivy slipped it behind her back and made her way downstairs.

In the doorway to the music room, she paused and studied the assembled guests.

Gertrude St. Martin was wearing a gown of deep rose watered silk, with a high neckline and long, tapered sleeves. At her throat twinkled a necklace of enormous diamonds, surrounded by rubies. In her earlobes were matching diamond and ruby earrings.

Standing at her side, Caine wore a black dinner jacket with a starched white shirt. His formal attire was such a dramatic change from his usual casual look, Ivy found herself staring.

Darren St. Martin and David Tisdale, both in formal tuxedos, were deep in conversation in the corner of the room. At her arrival, they looked up. David said something to Darren and began walking toward Ivy.

Standing in front of the fireplace, studying the picture that hung over the mantel, Diana was wearing a blue velvet cocktail suit. Her hair had been swept back dramatically, revealing small sapphire earrings.

Caine's head came up sharply, as if sensing Ivy's presence even before she approached.

"You prefer red wine," he murmured, handing her a crystal tulip glass.

"Thank you."

As she accepted it, their fingers touched. Caine glanced down into her face, loving the way she colored at his simple touch.

"I knew you'd be the most beautiful woman in the room."

Uncomfortable with his easy compliment, she changed the subject. "You look as if you'd been born to wear formal clothes."

"Not at all. But after Darren and I came here to live, Trudy insisted on it for every important occasion. Maybe that's why I wear jeans and old sweaters whenever possible."

"Hello, Ivy. Your presence here has just made this party much more interesting." David hurried to her side and caught her hand.

"Thank you, David. Where's your grandfather?"

He pointed. "Probably regaling the guests with stories about his youth. To hear him, he and Miss St. Martin were involved in more pranks than two dozen children."

At that moment, Gertrude looked up. "Ivy. Come here, child, and let me look at you."

Ivy walked to the sofa to stand before a beaming Gertrude.

"Oh, my dear. You're lovely. You do this company proud."

"Thank you, Aunt Tru. Happy birthday." Pulling her hand from behind her back, she handed the old woman a package.

As eager as a child, Gertrude tore the paper from the package to reveal a small portrait.

For long moments the old woman stared at the face in the portrait, then looked up. Through a mist of tears, she asked, "How did you know what I looked like as a young girl?"

"I asked Chester to send me a picture from your album. I thought you wouldn't mind if I borrowed it for a few weeks." She handed Gertrude an envelope containing the faded photograph.

Ivy was aware that Caine had stiffened beside her. Now he stared openly, as if really seeing her for the first time.

Relief flooded through him. So this was the conspiracy. Chester had stolen a photograph from Gertrude's album for a birthday portrait. He released his breath in a long sigh.

"Oh, Ivy, my dear. That was one of my favorites. And that dress. I still remember how beautiful I felt in it. You've captured everything; the sunlight on my hair, the delicate lace at my throat, the dreamy look in my eyes. How I'll treasure this. Thank you." She stood and pressed trembling lips to the young woman's cheek.

"I'm so glad you like it."

"I love it."

Turning, Gertrude motioned for the butler to place the picture on an end table for everyone to admire. The guests gathered around. While they were all too busy to take notice, Gertrude slipped from the room. A few minutes later she returned, holding a small leather case.

"I have the perfect accent for that dress, Ivy," she muttered, opening the case. "Caine, will you help me with this clasp?"

A gasp escaped Diana's lips as Gertrude held up a dazzling antique necklace of diamonds surrounding an enormous emerald.

"With your eyes and that dress, this will be stunning," the old woman said, as Caine slipped the necklace around Ivy's neck.

The touch of his cool fingertips sent little flames skittering along her skin. When he had secured the clasp, he allowed his touch to linger a fraction.

"Oh, yes. Perfect," Gertrude murmured, nodding approval. "What do you think, Caine?"

"Not even your emeralds do her justice, Trudy," he muttered, staring deeply in Ivy's eyes before turning away.

The old woman stared after him thoughtfully.

"I approve," Diana said, walking up to her daughter. "With a bit more makeup and a little more poise, you could probably be a model."

"I already have a career, Mother. I'm an artist, remember?"

"Art?" She nodded toward the landscape over the mantel. "You mean precious scenes from your childhood? Or copies of old photos? I doubt there's much market for such mundane things."

Ivy bit back the remark that sprang to her lips and walked away. The chasm between them widened. Soon there would be no crossing it.

Chester was kept busy answering the door and announcing guests. In her eighty years, Gertrude St. Martin had obviously made many friends. The guests reflected both her childhood here in the country, and her travels to New York and abroad. Their ages spanned nearly a century.

One maid did nothing but accept wraps as the guests arrived, and show the ladies to the powder room. In the music room, two maids circulated with trays, dispensing drinks and accepting empty glasses. A bartender, hired for the evening, mixed drinks in the corner of the room where a bar had been set up.

In the dining room, a buffet dinner had been arranged, with seating at round tables for ten in the adjoining glassed-in atrium.

During dinner, a small group of musicians assembled in the music room for late-night dancing.

Caine, Ivy noticed, stayed close to his aunt during the festivities.

"Sit with us, Ivy," David offered, holding a chair.

Accepting his invitation, Ivy sat down beside Jacob Tisdale.

"I was just telling my grandson and the others about the time Gertrude and I were coming up on the train from New York City," Jacob said to Ivy. "She was about seventeen and attending a prissy little boarding school at the time, and I considered myself a man of the world since I was in law school."

"I was sixteen," Gertrude corrected. "And you were embarrassed to have any of your friends see me with you." To Ivy she added, "They all teased Jacob about having to baby-sit me every time we both came up from the city for a weekend."

The old man's eyes glinted with humor. "The headmistress of her school usually would make sure that her students had a luncheon packed for the ride home. Gertrude was always such a rebel. One time, Gertrude actually went up and down the aisles of the train selling her food just to see how much she could earn."

"Of course," the old woman added, "Jacob was mortified. He said that if anyone we knew spotted me selling my lunch, the rumor would start that my father had lost his fortune and would spread like wildfire all through the countryside."

"Why did you sell your lunch, Aunt Tru?"

"Just to see if I could do it. I'd always admired the clerks in the stores for their independence. When I told Father that I wanted to work, he threw a fit. No woman in the St. Martin family would ever do such a thing, he insisted."

"So of course, you can guess what Gertrude did."

Ivy felt a kinship with the old woman, recalling some of the ways in which her own rebellion manifested itself. "You got a job?"

The old woman chuckled. "Sort of. It's odd that you should have mentioned modeling earlier, Diana. A fashion designer in New York spotted me when I was in buying a spring wardrobe, in my final year of high school. He asked me if I would be willing to wear some of his formal gowns at a charity benefit. I was so flattered."

"You said 'sort of,' Aunt Tru. What happened?"

Gertrude's eyes lit with the memory. "Nearly all of society was at the event. I glided out on the runway in a wicked gown of sheer ivory crepe. To accentuate the risqué dress, someone had thrust an elegant gold cigarette holder in my hand. To make things worse, I had forgotten to put on a slip, and in the bright lights you could see my legs clearly through the fabric. And it was just my luck that my father was in the crowd."

Darren looked puzzled. "What's wrong with a cigarette holder, for heaven's sake? And what could possibly be so terrible about seeing your legs?"

"In those days? Everything. A student in high school didn't openly smoke, or even look as if she did. And a lady always wore a heavy cotton petticoat beneath her dresses." She turned to a laughing Jacob. "You were there, too, to witness my humiliation. My father felt disgraced. He charged backstage like a wounded bull and threatened to haul me outside in my robe if I didn't dress immediately and go home with him."

To the others, Jacob said, "Of course, that only whetted Gertrude's appetite for even wilder escapades."

"Like what?" Ivy coaxed.

"In her first year of college, she dropped out of school to work for a young senator."

Ivy turned in time to see the look on the older woman's face. Though she hadn't moved, her expression was slightly altered. She seemed to be hardly daring to breathe.

"Do you remember, Gertrude?" Jacob asked.

His hostess nodded her head.

"He was the most exciting politican to come along in years. He had it all. A Harvard education, a moneyed family. He was single, handsome, charming. Everyone said it would be only a matter of time until he was president."

"What happened then, Aunt Tru?"

Gertude blinked, then turned to Jacob. Her voice had grown very soft. "It's your story. I'll let you finish it."

"When her father got wind of what had happened, he raced down to New York City to pick up his daughter and take her home." To Gertrude he muttered, "I'm sure he managed to shake some sense into that pretty head of yours." Jacob chuckled and turned to the others at the table. "Like a good girl, she dropped out of sight. The next I heard, she was off to a university in Europe. Four years later, she returned to dazzle our rather dowdy society. Gertrude St. Martin was the most beautiful, most sought-after young woman in the state of New York." His voice lowered. "I know she stole my heart. And I was never the same."

"Oh you." With misty eyes, Gertrude placed a hand over Jacob's. "You always did know how to flatter."

"It's the truth, and you know it. I would have married you in a flash, if you had only said the word."

For a moment Gertrude grew solemn. "Jacob, you were always so ambitious, I'm afraid I thought you were more in love with my inheritance than with me."

He glanced down, suddenly uncomfortable. "Perhaps when I was a callow youth. I've always valued wealth and its trappings. But when I matured, I yearned to have you say yes to my proposals."

"And have all your friends teasing you for the rest of your life about baby-sitting me?"

He joined in her laughter. "All those so-called friends of mine pursued you for years. I've always wondered, Gertrude, if anyone ever tempted you to give up your independence for love."

She was silent for long moments. Finally meeting his eyes, she said softly, "Allow an old woman a few secrets, Jacob."

"What happened to the senator?" Ivy asked. "Did he become president?"

"He died tragically," Jacob answered. "I believe a horse threw him. Do you recall, Gertrude?"

The old woman nodded her head. "He was riding in Central Park. They say he often went on lonely, brooding rides in the late afternoon. After the riderless horse returned to the stable, someone was dispatched to find the senator. He—" her voice wavered "—had broken his neck. He was dead before he arrived at the hospital."

Sensing her mood, Caine stood and caught her hand. "The musicians have started in the other room, Aunt Trudy. May I have the first dance?"

She gave him a grateful smile and took his arm. As they walked away, Jacob said, "She's still the finest-looking woman I've ever met."

He turned to Ivy. "Will you do me the honor, young lady?"

She smiled. "Thank you, Judge Tisdale. I'd love to."

Taking the old man's arm, Ivy walked to the music room and danced a slow, graceful waltz. When the song ended, they stopped to applaud the musicians.

"You're a very good dancer, Ivy. Most young people don't know how to move to slow music." Jacob turned to Gertrude. "But this lady is the best. Come on, Gertude. You owe me a birthday dance."

As the two old people moved away, Caine opened his arms. "Want to give it a try?"

She accepted his offer and stepped into his arms. With her hand lightly touching his shoulder, she felt a sudden thrill as his arm encircled her waist.

"You won't be as good a dancer as Judge Tisdale. But then, he's had years of practice."

"What I lack in skill, I'll make up for in other ways. For instance, can the good judge do this?" Caine ran a fingertip along the exposed skin of her back, and felt the shiver she tried to control. "Or this?" He bent his head, brushing his lips with feather-light strokes across her temple.

He could feel her pulse beat race at his touch.

She fought to keep her tone light. "Stick to your dancing, Caine."

"I am." He drew her firmly against him and moved to the music. As his lips pressed into a tangle of hair, she became achingly aware of the body that was imprinting itself on hers. She wished the music would go on forever.

"May I cut in?"

At the familiar deep voice, Ivy looked up into laughing blue eyes, the bluest eyes she had ever seen. The man, in his early forties, was tall, nearly as tall as Caine, with dark hair cut razor-short. His dinner jacket was beautifully tailored to fit his trim figure.

"Emery! Oh, what a wonderful surprise!" Ivy flew into his arms and kissed him warmly.

Caine stood stiffly beside her, his eyes narrowing at the easy familiarity between Ivy and the man.

"I had no idea you knew Aunt Tru."

"Aunt Tru, is it? I've known Miss St. Martin for years. She's bought several very good paintings from me."

"Emery, this is Caine St. Martin, Gertrude's nephew. Emery Norton owns the Norton Gallery, where I had my exhibit."

The two men shook hands, each taking the measure of the other.

"Hello, Caine. I believe you bought one of Ivy's paintings during the exhibit. You dealt with my assistant, Laura."

"That's right. Nice to meet you, Emery."

Ivy tucked her arm through Emery's. "If you had told me you were driving up from New York, I could have come up with you instead of on my bike."

"You rode that disgusting vehicle all this way? Now I know you're as crazy as all the other artists I deal with." He gave Caine a mock-pained expression.

"You have no idea what it's like, working with all these offbeat characters. Not one of them is completely normal."

"I've noticed," Caine said, meeting Ivy's grin. Emery dropped an intimate kiss on the top of her head. "If you can find some way to ship that bike home, you're welcome to drive back with me tonight."

"It's tempting." Her eyes danced. "But I think I'll just go home the same way I came here. On my trusty motorcycle."

Emery's arm encircled her waist. "Come on. You still owe me a dance."

As they twirled away, Ivy saw Caine turn toward the doorway. She couldn't see the flare of his nostrils, or the brooding look on his face. But the memory of his touch lingered.

The guests continued to arrive until the crowd swelled to over one hundred. Ivy's feet began to feel as if she had danced with every man at the party. As she took a break from the dancing and sipped a glass of wine, Darren caught her arm. Beside him stood a lovely young woman, with long, curly blond hair and lively hazel eyes. Her blue strapless gown displayed a luscious figure.

"This is Sara Davis."

Ivy smiled. "Hello, Sara. A friend of Aunt Tru?"

"Yes. I worked here during college to pay for my tuition."

"What do you do now?"

"I'm teaching at the local elementary school. Miss St. Martin has followed my progress since those years I worked here. I was delighted to be invited to her party."

How like Aunt Tru, Ivy thought.

"Your friend, Emery Norton, has just been telling me that you're a rich, successful artist, Ivy," Darren said. "I'm proud of you. I always knew you could do anything you set your mind to."

Ivy smiled and sipped the tart red wine. "Emery loves to embroider the facts."

"According to him, yours is a name to remember. Norton seems to think you'll go on to even bigger and better things." He caught her arm. "Come on. Let's dance."

"I thought you'd never ask." She put down her glass and allowed him to lead her to the dance floor. Over his shoulder she noted the blonde's look of disappointment and felt a momentary twinge of pity.

As they moved, Darren touched the emeralds at Ivy's throat. "If you play your cards right, I think you could persuade Aunt Gertrude to let you keep these. She's feeling so mellow tonight, she's in the mood to grant all kinds of unexpected favors."

"Don't be silly, Darren. What would I want with Aunt Tru's jewelry?"

"Are you kidding? Those stones are worth a fortune. I know jewelers who could sell them tomorrow."

"But the antique setting is priceless. The necklace has probably been passed down through generations."

He shook his head before twirling her dramatically. The skirt of her gown billowed about, then floated gracefully around her calves.

"Then ask her for them anyway and give them to me. I'll find a good use for them."

Ivy laughed. "You'd look smashing in emeralds."

"I know a great hock shop where I could get a pocketful of money for them."

"Don't talk nonsense, Darren. These are part of Aunt Tru's family collection. That means that some day they'll belong to you and Caine. You're her only heirs."

"Some day can be a long time."

"What's the hurry?"

The music ended. "I've always been a man in a hurry. Haven't you noticed?"

Ivy took his arm and walked from the dance floor. "Where are you hurrying to this time, Darren?"

He shrugged. "I don't know. Somewhere. Anywhere." His voice was suddenly bleak. "I want Melanie back."

His statement surprised her. "I thought she was off on some actor's yacht."

His eyes clouded. "I'll win her back. All I need is a break." He turned, and focused on Ivy. "How much can you get for a painting?"

She blinked at the unexpected question. "It depends. Each one is different."

"But give me an average. A hundred? A thousand? A hundred thousand?"

She was relieved when David Tisdale interrupted them.

"I've been waiting for my chance, Ivy. Let's dance."

She caught his hand and gave Darren a brilliant smile. "Catch you later."

"I'd been hoping to get you alone," David murmured as he and Ivy wove through the crowded dance floor.

Ivy gave him a dazzling smile. "I'm all yours."

She felt the dancer beside them stiffen, and found herself looking into Caine's gray eyes.

"I want to show you some of the countryside before you go back to New York. What have you planned for tomorrow?"

They turned, and the couple in front of them did the same. Over David's shoulder, Ivy faced Caine's dark look.

She licked her lips. "I really don't know yet, David. I guess I'll just have to wait and see what Aunt Tru has planned."

"I hope we have some time alone. There's so much I'd like to show you. Besides, I'd like to find something a little more private, so we could get to know each other better."

Caine's lips curled into the barest hint of a smile. But his eyes, she noted, were as cold as steel.

"Your friend, Emery Norton, said you were an important artist. I've always been interested in art. Maybe we could spend some time talking about it."

Ivy was beginning to find the evening interminable. When would it end?

"That would be nice, David."

His smile grew. "My grandfather has a fabulous collection of exotic automobiles. We drove up in an Excalibur in mint condition. Would you care to see it?"

"Now?"

"No. Tomorrow. I thought it would be a luxurious way to see the countryside. Of course, I'll have to ask my grandfather for the keys. He keeps a tight rein on them."

And the money, Ivy thought. And the law practice. And the people around him. She forced a smile. "Let's wait until tomorrow."

He drew her closer. "Fine, I can hardly wait."

When the song ended, Ivy saw Caine whisper in the ear of his partner. Ivy turned away, unaware of the cold, gray eyes that watched her as she stopped to laugh and chat with a cluster of friends.

Chapter Seven

It was after two o'clock in the morning before the musicians packed up their instruments and the last guest said good-night. Chester and the maids scurried about, picking up the party debris.

Judge Tisdale, leaning heavily on his grandson's arm, kissed Gertrude gently on each cheek. "Will you forgive me, Gertrude?"

"Forgive you? Whatever for?"

"For being old and foolish. For rambling so to-night. For bringing up the past."

She caught his hand. "The past is just that."

He met her gaze. "Is it? I wonder." He seemed to force a cheerfulness he didn't quite feel. "It was a wonderful party, my dear. We must do it again next year."

She patted his cheek. "Sleep well, Jacob."

"And you, Gertrude."

His slow, measured footsteps and the tap of his cane could be heard on the stairs as David helped him to his room.

Darren kissed his aunt. "Eighty, Aunt Gertrude. When are you ever going to grow old? Watching you tonight, I believe you'll live to be a hundred." Still holding a drink, he sauntered off to bed.

Diana finished her wine, handed the glass to a maid, then took Gertrude's hand. "A very nice party, Gertrude. Thank you for inviting me."

"It was my pleasure, Diana. It occurred to me that you didn't often get a chance to socialize while you and James lived here on the estate."

"One hardly invites one's gardener and his wife to social functions." Diana's clipped words caused Ivy to turn from the window.

"I suppose. But I never thought of your husband as simply the gardener. He was a fine man. I considered him a friend." Gertrude turned away before she said more than she intended. "Caine, I think I need a good right hand."

Immediately her nephew was at her side.

"Ivy, my dear." Taking Caine's arm, Gertrude crossed the room and grasped the young woman by the shoulders. Her features relaxed into a smile. "Every time I looked up, you were dancing with someone different."

Ignoring Caine's sudden scowl, Ivy smiled. "And what about you? You were as good as your word. You said you were going to dance until dawn at your party." She pointed at the inky sky. "Not quite dawn. But close enough."

Smiling radiantly, Gertrude gave the young woman a warm embrace. "Thank you again for the portrait. I shall treasure it."

"Then you'll forgive Chester for going through your album? He was so uncomfortable about doing that for me."

"I would forgive anything tonight. Now come and walk upstairs with us."

With Ivy on one side and Caine on the other, the old woman made her way slowly up the stairs. At Ivy's room, they stopped.

"Good night, Aunt Tru. It was a lovely party. Good night, Caine."

He nodded, then continued along the hallway, with Gertrude on his arm.

As Ivy closed the door to her room and crossed to the bed, she caught sight of her reflection in the dressing mirror. Seeing the emeralds, she fumbled with the clasp until it opened. For long moments she stared at the priceless necklace, loving the way light winked and reflected in the stones. A king's ransom. She was holding a fortune in diamonds and emeralds in her hands.

Hurrying down the hall, she tapped on the open door of Gertrude's bedroom, then rushed inside.

"I forgot to return the emeral..." Her voice died in her throat.

Gertrude was slumped in a chair, her face ashen, her eyes wide with fear. Beside her, Caine stood with his hands clenched at his sides. One hand was clutching a crumpled paper.

"Aunt Tru." Ivy flew across the room and dropped on her knees at the old woman's feet. "What's happened?" As soon as the words were out of her mouth, the realization dawned. "Oh, no. Not another letter."

Gertrude didn't move.

Ivy stood. "Let me read it, Caine."

His eyes were colder than she'd ever seen them. His face could have been carved from granite. He looked at her as if she weren't even there.

"Please, Caine. I want to read it."

"Stay out of this, Ivy."

Her eyes pleaded with him. "I'm already in it. Don't you see?" Her voice lowered to a whisper. "Trust me. Please."

He stared at her outstretched hand, then slowly held out the crumpled paper.

Like the others, the words had been cut from newspapers and magazines and pasted on plain, white paper. She read quickly.

I know about all the lies. Yours was not the greatest deceit. Someone close to you robbed you of the thing dearest to your heart. He didn't die. For one hundred thousand dollars, I will reveal the truth to only you, and keep your secret intact.

Still holding the letter, Ivy dropped on her knees and clutched Gertrude's icy hands in hers. "Does this letter make sense to you, Aunt Tru?"

For the first time, the old woman's voice sounded its age, faltering, tremulous. "Some of it."

Ivy looked up at Caine. "This letter demands one hundred thousand dollars. I'd say that's reason enough to call the police."

"No." Gertrude turned and clawed at Caine's hand. "No police."

"But why? Ivy's right. This is no longer just idle threats. This is a blackmail letter. A fortune, or they reveal your secret."

"Listen to me, Caine. This letter wasn't mailed. It was shoved under my door. There's no postmark on the envelope. That means someone who was here tonight sent it."

"Aunt Trudy," Caine said patiently, "you had over a hundred guests here tonight. The police can go through the guest list and determine how best to handle this."

"No. It's my secret. And my problem. I'll deal with it."

"No secret is worth that kind of money. Why not reveal it and be done with it? Then the blackmailer would have no reason to continue threatening you."

"This letter writer knows something I don't. Maybe that knowledge is worth it."

"A hundred thousand?" Caine's hands clenched at his sides. He resented his helplessness.

"Please, Caine. Let me think about this for a while. Tomorrow we'll talk."

"I'd like to keep this letter," he said.

"No. I want to read it over. Maybe it will make more sense to me when I'm not so tired." The old woman lifted herself from the chair and wrapped her arms around him. "Don't be angry with me, Caine."

He held her close. "I'm not angry, Aunt Trudy. I'm worried. This is not a simple matter."

"No. But it isn't life threatening either. What this person wants is my money, not my life."

He remained silent.

"Now please go. Both of you. I need to be alone."

Caine followed Ivy to the hall. He turned back to speak again to Gertrude. "Lock this door. And check your windows, too."

"I will."

"And keep the phone beside your bed."

She nodded. As the door closed, Caine waited until he heard the click of the lock. Satisfied, he turned away.

Ivy studied his firm profile. "What will you do, Caine?"

Distracted, he ran a hand through his hair. "I don't know." For the first time he noticed her pallor. "Go to bed, Ivy. There's nothing you can do tonight."

"I know I won't be able to sleep."

"Give it a try." He turned away.

Outside his room, Caine turned and watched until Ivy opened her door, entered, then closed it after her. He did the same.

In her bedroom, Ivy paced the floor. Who would do a thing like this? Someone deranged? No. That wasn't the answer. Aunt Tru said the letter made some sense to her. It had to be someone who knew a terrible thing about the old woman's past and was willing to expose it. And that someone was desperate.

Thoughts and images whirled through Ivy's mind. Distracted, she unbuttoned the sleeves of her silk gown, then slid it over her head and hung it in the closet. Kicking off her shoes, she dropped them on the floor of the closet. Clad in only the silk teddy, she began the pacing once more.

Why had she suddenly become attractive to Darren tonight? He had practically ignored her until now. Was it because Emery had told him she was a success? Could it be that Darren was a snob, who wouldn't waste his time with anyone unless she was wealthy or successful? Or—and the thought struck fear in her heart—was he so desperate for money that he would cultivate Ivy's friendship for that reason alone? If that was the case, would he also be desperate enough to resort to blackmail?

Oh, God. She covered her mouth, to stifle the oath that escaped. First she suspected her own mother. Now Aunt Tru's nephew and heir. What was happening to her?

What about Judge Tisdale? From the things he said tonight, he and Gertrude had known each other all their lives. There couldn't have been too many secrets in her past that he wouldn't know about. He seemed to genuinely care about her. Love. He had said he loved her, and she had rejected him. Would a spurned lover be driven to such desperate acts to even the score?

What of David Tisdale? As a lawyer, he had access to all the legal papers of Gertrude's family. His grandfather controlled David's career, his future, his very life. Would a young man trying to break free of such bonds resort to blackmail in order to win his independence?

A breeze ruffled Ivy's hair. Startled, she turned toward the locked door to the balcony. The curtains billowed inward. She could make out a pair of men's shoes standing just inside the door, behind the curtains.

Her eyes widened in terror. Her voice died in her throat. A hand pushed aside the fabric. Caine stepped toward her. He had changed from his formal attire to a pair of faded denims and a fisherman's knit sweater.

She felt her body tremble with relief.

"You scared me half to death. Haven't you ever heard of knocking?"

"I didn't want anyone to know I was here."

"How did you get that door opened? I checked the lock myself when I came in."

"I told you before. I've climbed these walls and broken into these rooms plenty of times when I lived here."

He stared pointedly at the teddy, which barely covered her nakedness. Then his gaze swept her body from her bare toes to her thighs, to the merest bit of silk on her hips. He studied her narrow waist, small enough for a man's hands to span. Then his gaze moved upward to her full breasts, clearly outlined beneath the pale silk.

"You'd better go."

"Not yet." His voice lowered. "I wanted you to know how happy I am about the birthday portrait."

"Why should that please you?"

He stepped nearer, until he could inhale the delicate fragrance of her perfume. "Because I overheard you and Chester earlier. I thought the two of you might be guilty of sending those letters."

She could feel the heat of his body. Defiantly, she lifted her head. "And now? Are you satisfied of my innocence?"

He reached a thumb and finger to the narrow spaghetti strap at her shoulder, feeling the smooth fabric against his rough skin. As his finger trailed the strap to the soft swell of her breast, he watched her eyes.

"Now I know that I was wrong to suspect you. You're probably the one person here this weekend who could never hurt Aunt Trudy."

She swallowed, forcing herself not to turn away from his dark gaze. "How can you be so sure?"

His finger dipped lower, to follow the deep V of the neckline.

"Because from the beginning I've seen a goodness, an integrity in your eyes that I've tried to deny. You've been telling the truth, Ivy. You're probably the only one who has."

Her mouth was dry. There was a dull ache at the back of her throat. She felt a terrible urge to cling to him and give herself up to the drugging need that was making her knees weak.

"Please go now, Caine."

"No." His eyes narrowed. He lifted his thumb and forefinger to her hair, allowing the strands to sift and fall. "Silk. Your hair is pure silk." Removing the comb from her hair, he watched as wave after wave drifted about her face and shoulders.

Ivy was unable to move, unable to turn away. All she could do was stand and watch his eyes as his touch turned her bones to liquid.

With a finger he traced the fine arch of her eyebrow. His fingertip glided over the softest skin he had ever felt. It moved along the curve of her cheek, then made a detour to follow the circle of her ear.

Mesmerized, she stared into his gray eyes. How had she ever thought them to be as cold as steel? They were warm, glowing, burning with a passion that he still managed to hold at bay.

His finger dropped to her mouth, and she instinctively parted her lips. He traced the outline of her full lower lip, then dipped his finger inside her mouth. She gave a little sigh and felt a rush of heat.

He was making love to her with only the merest touch. He traced the ivory column of her throat, and pressed his finger to the little pulse beat. It leaped at his touch and proceeded to beat a wild tattoo.

Watching her eyes, he ran a finger beneath the strap of her teddy, then slid it over her shoulder. He saw her eyes widen a fraction. Lifting his other hand, he caught the second strap and slipped it down too. She needed only to move and the little piece of silk would glide down around her hips.

He caught her chin and lifted her face for his inspection. Then his palm glided around to cup the back of her head.

She blinked, then stared boldly into his eyes, seeing herself reflected there.

"Do you know how much I want you? How much I've wanted you since I first saw you?"

The hand at her shoulder was rough, pulling her firmly against him. His fingers caught at a tangle of hair. The kiss, when at last it came, held no tenderness. His mouth savaged hers, kissing her as she'd never before been kissed. His lips, his teeth, his tongue held her enthralled, until all she could think about was the wild, dark, mysterious taste of him.

He smelled faintly of tobacco and Aunt Tru's favorite aged whiskey. Not even that potent drink could have the effect on her his kiss was having. She curled her hands into the front of his sweater, drawing him even closer.

Desire ripped through him, a raging flame, and he fought to bank the fire. He had thought of nothing but her all evening, and now that she was here in his arms, he wanted to take his time, to taste, to savor.

The hand at her shoulder moved down her back, holding her firmly against the length of him. Her skin was soft, so soft. He wanted to feel her skin grow hot and moist under his touch. He wanted to know every line, every curve of her body.

He'd never felt such a need for a woman. Yet all they had ever shared was a kiss. The taste of that kiss had lingered long after she had left his arms. Now he wanted more, so much more.

His hands moved along her back, touching, kneading, thrilling to the softness of her. Her breasts were flattened against his chest. He found their peaks, already hard with desire, as he ran his hands between their bodies.

He heard her gasp and thrilled to it. Need became raw desire, until he thought he would lose his control and slip over the edge of reason. He wanted to take her with him, until they both slid over the realm of sanity into madness.

Her hands glided around his waist, under his sweater. His skin was hot, damp. She needed to feel him, all of him, mouth to mouth, flesh to flesh.

When she buried her mouth against his throat, he felt her breath shudder over his skin. Everywhere she touched him he was on fire, and it was burning out of control.

She was his now, his completely. He felt her total surrender, and his heart soared at the knowledge. This strong, beautiful woman had surrendered to him.

His lips covered hers, nibbling, suckling, taking them higher and higher until he realized that her surrender was also his. He had lost himself in this woman, and no other woman would ever mean anything to him again.

Effortlessly he lifted her in his arms and carried her to the bed. With almost unbearable tenderness he settled her on the sheets, then stretched out beside her.

Ivy heard him groan her name before his lips covered hers. "Weed. My lovely little Weed."

His hands began a slow, rhythmic exploration of her body. She had no will to stop him. His lips, his hands were lifting her to heights she'd never known before. He leaned over her, dropping kisses on her wrist, the inside of her elbow, her upper arm. As he brought his mouth to the hollow of her throat, she felt light-headed, and deliciously weak. Looking up, she saw the glitter of desire making his eyes gleam silver in the lamplight.

There would be no turning back, she knew. They had both slipped over the line of reason. Needs pulsed and throbbed, driving them deeper into passion. Their bodies had become a mass of nerve endings, responding to each touch of lips and fingertips.

Ivy felt her body hum and soar, higher than she'd ever been before. The world dissolved. There was only this bed, and this man, the ecstasy of his touch, and the dark, mysterious taste of him.

They were so caught up in their lovemaking, they didn't hear the light tap on the door.

"Ivy? Are you in there?"

Caine's hands stilled. Ivy paused, praying she had only imagined the voice.

The knock sounded louder. "Ivy? I see your light. I need to talk to you."

It was a man's muffled voice. Darren's? David's?

She turned wide eyes to Caine. He leaned up on one elbow and traced the outline of her lips, swollen from his kisses.

"Send him away." His voice was a low growl against her mouth.

She wanted to cry in frustration. From the look on Caine's face, he shared her feelings.

"Who is it?" Ivy called softly.

"Darren."

"I'm sorry, Darren. I'm ready for bed. We'll talk in the morning."

"I'm afraid this can't wait. I have to see you now. I'll wait until you're decent."

Caine swore. His finger traced her eyebrow and he bent to place his lips to the spot. Her lids were heavy. Her eyes glowed, wide and luminous and softened with love.

"I'm not getting up, Darren. You'll have to see me in the morning."

The voice grew louder. "I'm not leaving until we talk. I'll wait right here until you open the door."

With a sigh of frustration, Caine sat up and caught Ivy's hand, helping her to a sitting position beside him.

He sucked in a long, ragged breath. "It seems the best laid plans..."

She nodded, feeling empty and desolate.

He stood and pulled her to her feet. Wrapping his arms around her, he kissed her, then turned toward the balcony.

"I'll leave the way I came in. And if any more men knock on your door tonight, you can have a steady stream of them going over the side of the house."

She chuckled, then blew him a kiss.

He strode across the room and pulled her roughly into his arms. "One last kiss to warm me through the night."

A flame, hot, and searing, leaped between them.

Without a backward glance, he stepped through the open balcony door and was gone.

Ivy rummaged through the closet and pulled on a modest robe before facing Caine's brother.

Chapter Eight

Ivy straightened the covers of her bed, smoothing the quilt and fluffing the pillow. She ran a hand through her tangled hair, then waited until her breathing was calm and steady. With a forced smile, she opened the door to admit Darren to her room.

He had removed his jacket but was still wearing the pleated tuxedo shirt and black pants with the narrow cummerbund. His tie was missing, and the shirtfront and cuffs were gaping open. His hair, always so perfect, was mussed, spilling over a forehead marred by a frown. Gone was the smug facade, the boyish charm. He was the picture of despair.

"I needed to talk to you without anyone knowing about it," he began, slumping into a chair.

"What's wrong, Darren?"

He clasped his hands between his knees. "I need to borrow some money, Ivy."

"Why?"

"There was a message in my room. Melanie is in Reno. She's filed for divorce. I need money."

"How much?"

"Fifty thousand dollars."

"Fifty—" She swallowed convulsively. "That's impossible. How could I come up with that kind of money?"

He hedged. "Emery Norton said you were a successful artist."

"But you don't understand what he meant. I equate success with feeling good about my work. The public, the art critics, are beginning to like what I do. I'm growing in my craft. Each year I feel stronger, more sure of what I'm doing. That's success, Darren. Not the amount of money I can command for a painting."

"Are you saying you can't come up with a few thousand dollars for a friend?"

"I don't have that kind of money."

"But you could. You could go to Aunt Gertrude."

"Why should I? Why don't you go to your aunt or Caine?"

"I've borrowed my limit from both of them."

"And never paid them back?"

He nodded. "I've tried. But every time I get some money saved, something comes up." He shrugged. "Melanie says spending money is twice the fun of saving it."

"And of course you always do everything Melanie says."

He glanced up at her. "It's easy for you to flaunt your independence, Ivy. You don't know what it's like to want someone so badly you ache."

He missed the look of pain that crossed her face.

"I miss her so much. I don't want to go on without her."

"It doesn't sound as if you can go on with her either, Darren. If you keep on this way, she'll turn you into a beggar, or worse." *Oh, Darren. What have you become?* Ivy thought. *A thief? A blackmailer?*

"I'd beg, to keep Melanie's love."

"Would you steal for her? Threaten people you love?"

At Ivy's sharp tone, Darren looked up. "What's wrong, Ivy? Why are you so angry?"

"I feel ashamed for you. And you should feel ashamed of yourself. Do you really believe Melanie left you because of money?"

"Of course."

"Then you're better off without her. Love, real love, would never have a price tag. If she really loved you, she'd want to be with you, have to be with you, no matter what. When two people love each other, it doesn't matter what their careers are, or how very different they may be in temperament." Her voice trailed off for a moment, as Ivy realized she wasn't lecturing Darren any longer. She was speaking to her own heart as well.

With Caine, she could be herself. He listened to her and understood what she was saying. He made her laugh, something she needed in her life. And in his arms, she felt a fulfillment she'd never known before. Despite the fact that they were very different personalities, she sensed that they would be good for each other. Only with Caine was she truly vital, vibrantly alive.

"Maybe she left you because you weren't man enough to stand up for what you believed to be right."

Darren stood and walked to the door. "This is exactly what I needed. Another lecture. All I'm asking is that you go to Aunt Gertrude and borrow some money for me."

"Why would she be willing to loan me money?"

"Just take my word for it, Ivy. She will."

She shot him a puzzled, angry look. "You're not making much sense tonight, Darren. Now let me get some sleep."

"You won't go to my aunt?"

"Certainly not. I have no intention of borrowing money for you. It's time you faced some responsibility."

"What happened to the sweet little Ivy I used to know? Years ago I used to be able to con you into doing my homework while I played football. I even managed to beat you at hockey sometimes."

Despite her dismay at his display of weakness, she walked up and put her arms around his neck. "I'd forgotten that. You really were a pro at getting other

people to help you out. That little girl you knew grew
up. I think you should do the same.''

Standing on tiptoe she kissed him lightly. "I know
that underneath it all you're a good man, Darren. I
suggest you pull yourself together and learn to stand
alone. Then, and only then, look for a good woman
to share your life.''

He seemed genuinely frightened by her words. "I've
never been alone, Ivy. There was always Caine, or
Aunt Gertrude, or Melanie. I'm not sure I can stand
to be alone, even for a little while.''

She opened the door. "You'll survive, Darren. And
you'll get to know yourself. And with some patience,
you might even discover strengths you never knew you
had. I'm willing to bet if you give it a chance, you'll
like the person you become.''

He kissed the tip of her nose. "I guess I have no
choice. I'm going to be alone whether I like it or not.''
Some of the old charm crept into his smile. "Do you
think you could at least loan me a couple of
hundred?''

"Oh.'' She gave him an exasperated shove into the
hallway and firmly closed the door.

As he walked away she could hear him chuckle.

She was glad she had made him smile for a few
minutes. But the truth was, she would have to tell
Aunt Tru what she suspected. Darren had seemed
desperate enough to resort to blackmail.

Peeling off her robe, Ivy snapped off the light and
crawled into bed. The bedside clock read four o'clock.
Practically dawn. With so many thoughts crowding

her mind, she wondered if she would be able to sleep for even an hour.

The sun was high in the sky before the figure in the bed stirred. Ivy squinted at the clock, then scrunched her eyes tightly shut. The bright light hurt. She hadn't believed it possible. She'd slept for six hours.

She showered and dressed quickly, then headed for the dining room. Spotting a maid carrying a tray to Aunt Tru's room, Ivy turned and followed.

The old woman looked up at the tap on her door. "Good morning, Martha. Just set it there, please," she said, indicating a round table by the window. "Oh, Ivy. Why don't you join me? I'm having a light breakfast here in my room."

"Thank you. I'd love to."

"Bring another juice, Martha, and some muffins."

"And a pot of coffee, please." Ivy's nerves were crying out for caffeine.

"How did you sleep?"

Ivy held the older woman's chair, then seated herself across the table. "Fine. Much better than I'd expected. How about you?"

Gertrude shook her head. "Badly, I'm afraid. The mind can be a terrible place to dwell, especially in the dark of the night."

Ivy poured coffee and noticed that Gertrude's hand shook slightly as she lifted the cup to her lips.

"My poor father," the old woman mused, as if he had been on her mind for quite a while. "I must have been a terrible burden on him," she muttered.

"Why do you say that?"

"I was only seven when my mother died," Gertrude explained. "He never seemed to know quite what to do with me after that. Here on the estate I grew to be a very undisciplined little girl. So he sent me off to a succession of boarding schools, guaranteed to turn little monsters into the very models of society. Each one admitted failure with me."

"But I've seen the pictures of you, Aunt Tru. You were a beautiful young woman, elegantly dressed, perfectly poised."

"Ah, yes. I always managed to look the part. But the truth was, there was a wild streak in me that my father refused to accept. He felt that the perfect daughter should be docile."

Ivy smiled. That was one word that would never describe Gertrude St. Martin.

"My father demanded that I live by not only the laws of society, but his even stricter rules as well. He would tolerate no disobedience. As you can imagine, I thought my father was perfect." Her voice lowered slightly. "When I returned from my schooling in Europe, my father introduced me to my new stepmother. She was one of the teachers from my high school. A young woman, barely older than I."

Gertrude set down the cup with a clatter. Her voice was strained. "Can you imagine my shock that they had kept this attraction a secret from me? My puritanical father, so perfect, so unapproachable, and a teacher from my former school? Was this the man who had demanded perfection and blind submission from his daughter?'' She touched a napkin to her lips. "I'm afraid I behaved rather badly. I had imagined that I would return from Europe to be the mistress of the house. Instead, I had to take a back seat to a young woman, barely out of her teens. And then they had a child.''

Ivy met her look. "Your sister, Jenny.''

"Half sister. Yes. My stepmother died in child-birth. And I found myself in the strange position of having everything I'd ever wanted. I was now mistress of this fine house, and free to raise the baby as I pleased. My father tried, in his own strange way, to be a father to Jenny. But he was too tired, too defeated. I was actually both mother and father to her.''

"It must give you great satisfaction to know that you could give your father the help he needed.''

The old woman stared out the window, lost in thought. "Jenny was delightful, though my father never really noticed. He died an embittered old man, angry at being robbed of his second chance for happiness. I'm afraid there had been too much anger between us to ever leave room for such things as love and forgiveness.''

"At least you haven't been childless after all.''

Gertrude met her look. Ivy was shocked at the pain she could read in those depths.

"No. I wasn't childless. There was Jenny. And when she announced, at eighteen, that she was going to marry a widower with two sons, I gave her my blessing, even though I thought she was very young to take on such responsibilities.'' The old woman's voice trembled. "It seems to be a St. Martin curse. She had only two years of happiness."

"And you found yourself with two more children to raise."

Gertrude's eyes softened. "Caine and Darren. My sister's stepchildren."

Both women looked up at the knock on the door. The maid entered with another tray.

"Thank you, Martha."

"Will there be anything else, Miss St. Martin?"

"No. Thank you. Is my nephew Caine up yet?"

"Yes, ma'am. He left an hour ago."

"Left? Where did he go?"

"He didn't say."

"When he returns, tell him I'd like to see him."

"Yes, Miss St. Martin."

When the door closed, Ivy poured fresh coffee. "What would have happened to Caine and Darren if you hadn't adopted them?"

"I checked. There was no other family." The old woman shrugged. "An adoption agency, I suppose. But there was never any question of whether or not I wanted them." She folded veined hands in her lap. "Right from the start, they were so different. One so careless, so sure everything would always be taken care of; the other so precise, so careful of every little detail. Darren reminded me of myself as a child. Caine was more like the person I'd had to become in order to survive. The weak and the strong. There seems to be a little of both in all of us."

Now was the time, Ivy thought, to tell Aunt Tru what she suspected about Darren. If she was wrong, though, she would feel terrible about destroying his aunt's faith in him. But if what she suspected was true, his aunt had a right to know in order to defend herself against his threats. While she debated with herself, the moment passed.

"Caine was the most fiercely independent child I'd ever known," Gertrude said. "He always insisted on doing everything for himself. The first summer he was in high school, he came home to announce he had a job working for a building contractor. Every summer of high school and college, he hauled bricks and blocks, roofing supplies, anything his employer wanted. He would come in on hot summer nights and collapse into bed, too tired to even eat. I watched him rub oil into hands all rough and callused, and my heart went out to him."

At her words, Ivy could feel the scrape of those work-roughened hands on her skin, and gave an involuntary shiver.

"When he apprenticed with an architectural firm, he refused to take a cent from me, living instead in a tiny little apartment in New York with two other roommates. And when he finally started his own firm, I know he barely scraped by. But he refused to take any help from me. He's such a proud, determined man." Her eyes shone. "And I'm so proud of him."

"Who are you proud of?" Caine stood framed in the doorway. Seeing their surprise, he explained, "I knocked. But you two were so busy with girl talk, you didn't bother to answer. So I let myself in."

"You seem to be an expert at that," Ivy said.

"At what?" Gertrude looked confused.

"At letting myself into rooms without knocking." He gave Ivy a dark, knowing gaze before he crossed the room and planted a warm kiss on the old woman's cheek. "How did you sleep?"

"At least I attempted to sleep, which is more than I can say for you."

Ivy felt her heart leap as she studied his craggy features, noting the dark stubble of beard he hadn't yet bothered to shave, the red-rimmed eyes.

"Have you had breakfast yet?" his aunt asked.

"No. I noticed a breakfast buffet being set up in the dining room."

"I suspected everyone would sleep late this morning. Including the staff. So I thought a buffet would take care of everyone nicely."

Caine nibbled a piece of his aunt's toast. "I'll shave first and make myself presentable. Then I'll join the others."

"Where were you off to so early in the morning?"

His face lost all expression. "I had some errands to run."

"On a Sunday morning?"

"Umm." He finished the toast and gulped a glass of juice. "I'll leave you two to your talk and go get cleaned up."

As he sauntered from the room, Ivy muttered, "Evasive."

"Independent," Gertrude amended.

"Whatever; he managed to tell us nothing."

"And you can bet that if that's the way Caine wants it, that's the way it will be."

Not if I can help it, Ivy thought as she bent to brush her lips across the old woman's cheek. "Thanks for the breakfast and the conversation," she murmured. "There was something else I wanted to tell you, but I think it can wait. I'll see you downstairs in a little while."

"Ivy." The old woman caught her hand. "Before your mother leaves today, try to talk to her."

"What about?"

The blue eyes were grave. "About your life, your career, your successes, your dreams."

"She isn't interested, Aunt Tru. I can't conform to what she wants for me."

"She loves you, Ivy. She just doesn't know how to tell you."

"Odd. I hadn't noticed."

"Oh, Ivy. Don't wait until it's too late."

"Aunt Tru," Ivy said patiently. "Maybe, like you, there's a touch of the rebel in me. I can't live up to her image of the perfect daughter."

"At least try to make peace."

Ivy stared at the hand which held hers. "At what price?"

"Just try. It will be worth a great deal to you one day."

Ivy nodded. "I suppose one more attempt won't hurt."

The old woman squeezed her hand. "Good."

As she made her way to her room, Ivy wondered about Gertrude's determination to make peace between a mother and daughter. Maybe regrets were the hardest things of all to live with.

Chapter Nine

It was one of those perfect spring mornings. The sky was a cloudless blue. A gentle breeze carried the intoxicating scent of early lilacs. Ivy shielded her eyes from the glare of the sun and watched a pair of ducks make a lazy circle in the air, then land effortlessly on the smooth water of the pond.

Leaving the flagstone path, she veered into the wooded area behind the pond. The secluded woods were alive with sound. Birds chirped. Frogs croaked. Insects hummed. Shoving her hands deep into the pockets of her jeans, Ivy filled her mind with the sights and sounds of the place. She might never get another chance like this, to explore this wonderful old estate that owned her heart.

She bent to examine a tiny blue flower and wished she'd brought her sketch pad. Straightening, she turned back toward the house.

As she emerged from the woods, she spotted a movement on the upstairs balcony of the house. Something fluttered in the breeze. Probably a maid shaking a rug, she thought.

As she circled the pond, she continued to stare, trying to make out what the figure was doing. By the time she was close enough to see clearly, it had disappeared. The balcony was empty.

Ivy quickened her pace. The long walk had sharpened her appetite. She was looking forward to a hearty breakfast.

As she paused in the doorway of the dining room, Ivy noted that only Caine and Gertrude were downstairs ahead of her. They were seated on a small love seat in front of French doors that opened onto a lovely terrace. Their heads bent closely together, they were engaged in earnest conversation.

"...leaving today. I'm willing to bet that before lunch, our letter writer will make a move."

Caine's head came up sharply, as if sensing Ivy's presence.

"I'm sorry. I didn't mean to eavesdrop."

"It's all right, child. Come in."

Ivy crossed the room to stand in front of them. "You're not going to pay the money, are you?"

The old woman smiled gently. "I couldn't possibly come up with that kind of cash."

Ivy let out a long sigh of relief.

"Of course, if they're willing to take jewelry, stocks, bonds, I could probably manage."

"Aunt Tru."

The old woman leaned forward to pat her hand reassuringly. "I'm only thinking out loud. I have no intention of giving in to blackmail."

"Then you've called the police?"

Gertrude glanced at Caine. "I don't think this is a matter for the police. I think this can be handled without them."

Ivy swallowed. "Aunt Tru, there's something I think you should know. Last night, I had a visitor."

Caine stood and touched her shoulder. To his aunt, he said, "Your guests are arriving for breakfast."

"Good, I'm ready for something a bit more solid myself." Gertrude took Caine's hand and stood. Squeezing Ivy's arm as she moved past her, she whispered, "We'll talk later, child."

Jacob was the first to arrive, leaning heavily on the arm of his grandson. The old man looked dapper in a dark suit, crisp white shirt and bright silk tie and handkerchief in his breast pocket.

His grandson wore a dark suit as well. His only concession to the casual mood of the morning was the lack of a tie.

Watching them, Ivy thought that the only thing missing were their briefcases.

David's eyes lit up at the sight of Ivy.

"You will go riding with me today, won't you?"

"We'd have to go right after breakfast. I'd like to get an early start back to New York."

Jacob's head came up as he accepted a cup of coffee from a maid. "Where are you two going?"

"I wanted to show Ivy some of the countryside before she left."

"And just what did you intend to drive?"

Ivy saw the slight flush that stained David's cheeks.

"David said you drove up here in an Excalibur, Judge Tisdale. I've never seen one before. So, he generously offered to take me for a ride."

"Did he now?" The old man's eyes met his grandson's. "That's a very expensive piece of machinery."

"I doubt there's much traffic on a day like this," Ivy said quickly.

The old man considered. "Yes. I suppose you're right. Why not? Enjoy the day while you can, David."

The young man flashed a brilliant smile. "Thank you, Grandfather."

Across the room, Ivy felt Caine's dark eyes boring into her. She tried to ignore the stab of regret. She hadn't wanted to spend any time with David Tisdale. But she resented the way his grandfather controlled him.

Caine watched David smiling down into Ivy's face. His eyes narrowed a fraction. Her lips were upturned and slightly parted. Her eyes when she laughed were the green of the sea. He could smell the fragrance of her delicate perfume. David touched her arm and whispered something. Caine's hands tightened at his sides. He was jealous. It was a feeling that was almost alien to him. What had this woman done to him? He was a man who always kept his emotions in check. During the short time he'd been with Ivy, he had experienced fury, desire, jealousy, and one thing he was afraid to even allow himself to give a name to—love.

The thought was so shocking he could only stand numbly and stare at the woman who had stolen his heart. No other woman would every satisfy him now. He wanted her. Wanted to spend the rest of his life with her. Love. The thought left him stunned and shaken.

Diana entered the dining room wearing white linen slacks and a peach silk shirt, with a mandarin collar and long, pleated sleeves. With her blond hair and tiny figure, the pastels made her look like a dainty confection.

In sharp contrast, Ivy studied her own faded jeans and simple cotton shirt, unaware of how they flattered her long legs and slender, youthful figure. She knew only that her mother would be appalled at her careless disregard for appearance.

Darren was the last to arrive for breakfast. He looked slightly better than he had the night before. Wearking khaki pants, a crew-neck cotton sweater and a pair of Italian leather loafers without socks, he still managed to give the impression of a playboy on the prowl. His eyes looked weary, but his smile was in place.

"I hope everyone slept well," Gertrude said as she filled a plate and carried it to a table on the terrace.

"Like a baby," Jacob muttered, following suit.

The others took their time, looking over the assortment of fresh fruits, eggs and sausages, cold meats and pastries.

On the terrace, a maid circulated, pouring coffee and juices.

Ivy took a seat between Caine and Darren. Across the table, Diana gave a small frown of disapproval.

"Did I understand Gertrude to say that you drove all the way up here on a motorcycle?"

"It's all right, Mother. I'm a very good driver."

"But what will you do if it rains?"

"Pull on a rain cape."

"Oh, Ivy. Don't you think you've carried this off-the-wall artist pose a little too far?"

Embarrassed at the sudden silence at the table, Ivy fought to keep her voice steady. "We'll talk about it later, Mother. I'd like to see you alone before we leave."

"What about?" Diana was suddenly suspicious.

"We'll talk, Mother. I promise. Before we leave today."

Ivy ducked her head and ate her breakfast in silence. Everyone, it seemed, was under a great strain this morning.

As soon as they finished second cups of coffee, David eagerly escorted Ivy to the garage, where he proudly showed off his grandfather's car. The low-slung bronze car, with gleaming chrome, had been carefully polished since their arrival from New York.

David held the door. "Isn't she a beauty?"

"Yes." Ivy laughed as David turned on the ignition. "Why do we refer to cars as she?"

"Because to a collector they're as sleek and sensuous as a beautiful woman."

"And are you a collector?"

He gave her a look before starting down the long, curving driveway. "Not yet. But soon, I hope."

"Does your grandfather allow you to drive his cars often?"

"As I'm sure you've noticed, my grandfather believes that what he has worked for is his alone. I have to prove myself before I can enjoy the fruits of his labors."

"How will you prove yourself?"

Leaving the private driveway, David turned onto the highway and floored the gas pedal. The sleek car flew along the pavement. "By working long hours for no pay. By seeing to my grandfather's every need. By dancing to the tune that he plays."

"He's lucky to have you, David."

The car hurtled faster along an open stretch of highway. When the road curved, Ivy felt the first thrill of fear. With a laugh, David pressed down even harder on the pedal, until they were nearly flying.

With the top down, the wind clawed at Ivy's hair, flailing it across her face, then whipping it out behind her in a long, dark stream. David's fine hair dipped and fell on the wind, making him appear even younger, more fragile.

It was impossible to talk while the car sped along the highway. The words would have been torn from their mouths and carried away on the wind. Ivy's heart raced as she watched David's hands on the wheel of the car. Their safety, their lives, depended on him. The look on his face was one of pure joy. Ivy suddenly realized what this speed meant to him. This was freedom from his grandfather's domination. This was control of his own life. This was release from the pressures of always having to live up to someone else's expectations. This was David's form of rebellion.

As last, he slowed the car and drove at a normal speed.

"Did you ever think about becoming a race driver?"

David laughed. "My grandfather would never have allowed it."

"I think you should consider it. That was some display."

"Are you afraid of speed?" he asked quietly.

"No. As a matter of fact, I like it. When I'm doing the driving."

"Did your mother tell you that she called me a few weeks ago?"

Ivy's head swiveled sharply at this unexpected twist in the conversation. "No. Why should she do that?"

"She was looking for some of your father's papers. Grandfather's firm has handled all the legal work for your father's family since they first came here."

Ivy felt her mouth go dry. "What kind of papers?"

"Just some legal papers. We have copies of everything from the time your grandparents first started as tenant farmers and caretakers for Miss St. Martin's father.''

"Why would my mother need those papers?''

He shrugged. "I don't know. I didn't ask.''

"Did you get her the papers she wanted?''

He nodded. "Sure. It took a little digging, but I came up with them. Odd,'' he said, chuckling, "all my work seems to come in bunches. The same day your mother called, Darren stopped by.''

"I thought Darren was in California.''

"He was, earlier. But he came up to New York for several days.''

"Does Aunt Tru know that?''

"I doubt it. He said he was staying with friends in New York.''

Everyone, Ivy realized, had had a chance to mail those terrible letters from New York.

"He just drove up to talk to me about a land deal.''

"Land?''

David slowed the car, then brought it to a smooth stop. Reaching out, he caught a strand of Ivy's hair. Avoiding her eyes, he watched the way her hair lifted in the breeze. "Darren and I talked to a developer about his aunt's property. It seems they'd be willing to pay a fortune to develop her land into a subdivision. That's prime land she's living on.''

"Aunt Tru would never sell.''

David ran a hand along Ivy's arm, feeling the slight chill from the rush of cold air. "That's what I found out when I approached her about the deal.''

She let out a long sigh. "So you've given up on the idea."

"For the time being. Of course, she can't live forever. But in the meantime, there are other ways to make a dollar." He lifted his arm to the back of the seat. "Slide over here and I'll keep you warm."

"No. I'm fine." She glanced at her watch, wishing she'd never agreed to this outing. "We'd better get back, David. I still have to pack."

"I'm going to be coming up to the city soon, Ivy. And when I do, I'd like to see you."

She should have known where this would lead. Trying for a note of enthusiasm, she said, "That would be nice, David. Give me a call."

"Caine St. Martin isn't the only man who has achieved success, Ivy. I intend to be very wealthy. I could show you a good time."

She blushed, remembering that David had seen her in Caine's bedroom.

Something clicked in her mind. "How are you planning to earn all this money?" Her heart nearly stopped, waiting for his reply.

"I have plans, Ivy. A lawyer learns a lot of things about his client's business."

The band around her heart tightened. "Let's go back now. Please."

"You will let me see you in New York?"

She swallowed. "Just give me a call."

He smiled, glanced at his watch, then started the car. Within minutes, they were at the private driveway leading to the St. Martin estate. As soon as she could politely get away, Ivy fled up the stairs. Outside Gertrude's room, she knocked.

"Come in."

"Aunt Tru. We have to talk."

"Not now, Ivy." The old woman's voice quavered. "The rendezvous is set. The note was under my door after breakfast. I'm to leave the money at the gardener's cottage. The note said I'll be watched. I'm to go alone. When the money is delivered, I'm to return to my room. The blackmailer promised a packet of documents and information about my past, some of which I have kept secret for a lifetime, and some of which I apparently never knew."

"You said you didn't have that kind of cash here in the house."

"I don't. Caine knew how distraught I was. He went to our banker this morning. He drew up a cashier's check for one hundred thousand dollars. Anyone can cash it at any bank."

"You're not going. You'll be hurt."

"Ivy." The old woman stood and took her cold hands. "I have to go. I have to know what this person knows about my past."

Ivy snatched her hands free and ran to the door. "I'm going to find Caine, and talk some sense into him. He'll stop you from going into a trap."

"Caine has already said he approves."

Ivy turned. Her face mirrored her shock. "I don't believe it."

"Then ask him. He said he understands what this means to me. And he wants me to see it through to the end."

Ivy's face darkened with fury. "Where is he?"

Gertrude shook her head. "I have no idea. You can try his room."

Ivy hurried down the hall and pounded on Caine's door. When there was no response, she turned the knob and let herself in. The room was empty.

She had to find him. She had to get him to stop his aunt from this meeting with a blackmailer.

As she moved past her room, the door opened and a hand was clamped over her mouth. She was unceremoniously hauled inside and thrown roughly up against the wall. With one hand the door was closed and locked.

She found herself staring into Caine's scowling face. His gray eyes were bleak and his slanting black eyebrows drew together to form a deep frown.

"You went for your ride with young Tisdale."

"Yes. Caine, I have to talk to—"

"And were you impressed by his expensive automobile?"

"Don't be silly. I—"

His hands thrust into her hair, pulling her head back. "And did he tell you how much he admired you, and wanted to see you again?"

"Caine, stop this. I have important—"

"And did you tell him to call you when you got back to the city?"

She swallowed. "Yes, but—"

Slate-gray eyes met hers. Eyes that were cold and ruthless. His fingers moved to the buttons of her blouse. "Last night we started something. Today I intend to finish it."

One by one he undid the buttons, all the while watching her eyes. Caught in the hypnotic spell of his steel gaze, she was powerless to stop him. He slipped the cotton shirt from her shoulders. Beneath it, she wore only an ivory silk chemise.

"Silk," he breathed, running a finger along the narrow strap. "Silk against your flesh." He ran an open palm across her shoulder. "Your flesh against mine. I've thought of nothing else."

His mouth crushed down on hers, shutting off the protest she was about to make. Passion caught them both by surprise. His arms came around her, molding her tightly to him, until she could feel the wild thunder of his heartbeat through her skin.

She caught him by the shoulders, clinging as if afraid to let go. She felt the blood pounding in her temples.

His hands moved along her back, caressing, kneading, feeling the softness of silk and the even-softer skin beneath.

He wasn't gentle. She had always known he wouldn't be a gentle lover. His rough hands moved along her sides, then upward to her breasts.

"Soft. You're so soft," he breathed inside her mouth.

Heat became flame, consuming them.

On a moan, she tightened her grip on his shoulders, knowing that if she let go, she would sink to the floor. Her legs could no longer support her.

While his hands worked their magic, touching her as no man had ever dared touch her before, he ran hot, moist kisses along the column of her throat.

She arched herself in his arms, loving the feel of his lips on her skin. Her body ached to be touched by those work-roughened hands.

"Caine, this is madness."

"Yes. Yes." His lips moved to her ear, where he nibbled the lobe, then darted his tongue with hot, quick thrusts.

He found her lips eager, parted, and covered them with a searing kiss.

Ivy had never known this raw hunger for any man. She was his. She could no more deny the need for him than she could stop breathing. She would give him anything he asked. There was nothing she could deny him.

As his lips moved over her throat, his name was a sigh on her lips. "Caine. Oh, Caine. We have to stop this. You know we have to."

"Why?" He lifted his head, then kissed her again. His voice was a raw whisper against her lips. "Why?"

"Because Aunt Tru is alone. And she needs us."

A grandfather clock in the hallway chimed the hour. He stiffened. Pressing his lips into a tangle of her hair, he held her against him. Both of them were struggling to calm their ragged breathing.

"What's come over me? I need to think." He felt the press of her body against his, and fought the overwhelming desire to touch her again.

With her, he lost all control. At a time when his aunt needed him, he was selfishly thinking about his own needs. He had nearly taken her there, in broad daylight, on the floor of her room. What was happening to him?

He drew in a long, burning breath. "Just stay here, out of the way. I have to get to that cottage ahead of Trudy. I know a place where I can hide and see everything that goes on inside."

"Like hell." He blinked at her unexpected outburst. "We're in this together. I have no intention of staying in my room while you and Aunt Tru face a blackmailer."

He caught her roughly by the shoulders and backed her against the wall. "You're staying here where you're safe. There's no telling what the blackmailer will do when confronted."

"I'm going with you. And nothing you can say will stop me."

He stared down into those fierce green eyes and knew defeat.

He let out a long sigh. "All right. Come along. And, Weed, remember. We're going to stay out of sight so we can catch a blackmailer. Try not to knock anything over."

"When this is finished, you're going to pay for that remark."

Chapter Ten

With Caine leading the way, Ivy plunged into the dense woods behind the pond.

"It's a lot longer this way, but no one can see us. Stay close," he cautioned.

They slipped from brilliant sunshine to an eerie world of filtered light and shadow. Giant evergreens towered above them, blotting out the sky. The trees grew so close together, that in spots, their branches were interwoven, like arms linked. Footsteps were cushioned by dirt and layers of pine needles. Their nostrils were assaulted by the dank scent of moist earth and the sharp, distinctive aroma of evergreen.

As they moved deeper into the woods, the shadows were more pronounced. They had entered a world of perpetual twilight. Above them the forest towered like giant cathedral spires, and even the normal nature sounds seemed hushed. Few birds except owls preferred the darkness. Even the usual hum of insects was absent.

Ivy had the strangest feeling that if she cupped her mouth and shouted, her voice would bounce off the giant trees, echoing and reechoing throughout the forest.

Caine stopped to get his bearings, and Ivy was grateful for the chance to rest against the trunk of a tree. The rough bark felt cool and slightly damp against her back. As they started up again, she stared at the width of Caine's shoulders. He was a strong man. But it wasn't his physical strength that impressed her. There was about him an inner strength that she had sensed from their first encounter. He was a man of great integrity. He had a strong sense of loyalty toward those who depended on him. He would never let them down. She instinctively trusted him. Though Ivy was frightened for Aunt Tru, and worried that the secrets from her past would cause her pain, she felt no fear for herself. She somehow knew Caine would never let her be hurt.

Deep in thought, she stiffened when his hand dropped to her shoulder. Her eyes widened. He lifted a finger to his lips to signal silence.

"We're almost there. When we enter the clearing, we'll be at the rear of the cottage. I'm going to run across that open space first, and check to be certain we're alone. When I wave, run as fast as you can to the back door."

She nodded.

Caine stood at the edge of the clearing, looking left and right. From a canopy of vines, she watched his lean, muscled figure streak across the clearing and disappear inside the cottage. For long minutes she waited, her heart racing. At this very moment he might have startled the blackmailer inside the building. They could be struggling. Caine could need her. She clamped damp palms together and lifted her fingertips to her lips in a prayerful attitude. She'd promised to wait for his signal. She strained to see the back door, afraid to even blink.

After what seemed an eternity, she saw Caine's figure appear at the door. He waved. Glancing about first, she dashed across the clearing and stepped inside the cottage. Taking long gulps of air, she followed him from the small laundry-workroom, through the kitchen and into the living room.

"Where will we hide?" she asked.

"When I was looking over the cottage, I noticed a small loft up there." He pointed to the far side of the room.

"Yes. My father built it for me. I used to call it my studio. Come on." She grabbed his hand, but he resisted her.

"I couldn't find a way up there," Caine complained.

"That's because we kept the ladder in here." Ivy opened a small panel in the wall and slid out a rough, handmade ladder.

She leaned it against the loft and led the way up, with Caine following. Then she pulled the ladder up and placed it against the back wall.

Caine glanced around the small loft. It was no larger than eight by ten feet, and carpeted in thick tweed shag. A wide wooden railing ran the length of it. It would be possible to sit behind that railing and see everything without being seen. Above them was a skylight. Below them the entire lower level of the cottage was spread out.

"I don't want you to speak, Ivy. Not even a whisper. I suspect the writer of those letters will be feeling very jumpy. I don't want any hint that we're here, or we just might scare off our blackmailer."

She nodded.

"Get as comfortable as you can. You may have to stay in one position for a very long time."

She sat down, leaning back against the wall. With just the turn of her head, she could see in any of three directions below. At her side, Caine sat and lifted her fingers to his lips.

She sat in silence, achingly aware of the man beside her. Though he didn't speak, his thoughts were mirrored in his eyes. He was remembering the simmering passion that he had unleashed by a simple touch. It was still there, smoldering between them, waiting for release.

The front door opened. Caine dropped Ivy's fingers. She felt him tense beside her.

Gertrude stood in the doorway, staring around. Cautiously she entered, then walked to the fireplace.

For the first time today, Ivy realized that the stone had been removed, revealing the small safe. Taking an envelope from her pocket, Gertrude thrust it into the recess in the stone, as she had been directed in the note, then placed the cutout stone over the hole. Giving one last glance around, the old woman strode briskly from the cottage, carefully closing the door behind her.

Ivy turned toward Caine. He held a finger to his lips. She nodded.

The next twenty minutes seemed an eternity. Just when Ivy had begun to relax, she heard a sound—a loud tapping sound on the flagstone walk. A moment later, the front door was thrust open. Ivy's hand flew to her mouth to stifle a gasp. She stared down in horror at the figure of her mother.

Diana paused in the doorway to allow her eyes to adjust to the gloom of the house, made darker after a walk in the bright sunshine. She walked across the room, staring at the fine, old leaded windows, running a hand along the neglected wood paneling. For a moment she sat on the hearth and touched a hand to the rough stones of the fireplace. Ivy held her breath as her mother gazed upward, staring at the wood-beamed ceiling. Then she crossed to the kitchen, where they could hear her footsteps echo on the tile floor. A few minutes later, Diana again entered the living room. After gazing at the fireplace for long moments, she walked to the hallway that led to the bathroom and bedrooms. Ivy could hear her mother's footsteps as she paused, first at Ivy's old room and then at the master bedroom. It was then that she heard the sound.

It started softly, like the wind sighing in the trees. As it grew louder, Ivy turned wide, horrified eyes to Caine. Her mother was crying. Sobbing her heart out. She was grieving. Something long forgotten stirred in Ivy. She remembered her mother dry-eyed beside the coffin. Though Ivy had wept until she thought her heart would break, Diana had remained unemotional throughout the entire ordeal of her husband's long illness and death. She had kept it all inside. And now, something had triggered the love and grief that she'd denied.

Ivy longed to comfort her. As she made a move to stand, Caine's hand clamped around her wrist.

"I have to go to her."

"No." The word was curt. "You can't move."

Only when he felt her acquiescence, did he release his hold on her.

Drawing her knees up, Ivy rested her chin and closed her eyes, wishing she could soothe her mother's pain. Beside her, Caine never moved.

When Diana emerged from the bedroom, she was dabbing a handkerchief to her eyes. With one last lingering look around the old cottage, she opened the door and walked out.

"Then she isn't the one." Ivy let out a long sigh of relief and felt her hands tremble.

Caine dropped an arm around her shoulder and drew her close. Once again, they began the agony of waiting.

When the front door opened a second time, there was no warning sound in advance. Ivy felt Caine stiffen beside her. They both stared down at the figure of Darren as he walked quickly into the room. Ivy turned to see the look of stunned disbelief of Caine's face. Slowly the look was replaced by one of bleak despair.

"Ivy," Darren called loudly. "Caine. Anyone here?"

Caine laid a hand on Ivy's arm to caution her into silence.

Darren strode from the room into the kitchen. A moment later he returned, then walked down the hallway. "Ivy. Caine. You here?"

His voice sounded hollow in the empty house.

"I'd sure like to know where everyone disappeared to today," he grumbled.

Pulling the front door open, he stepped out into bright sunlight and firmly closed the door behind him.

Ivy turned toward Caine and saw the relief shudder through him. He gave her a weak smile, then dropped his face into his hands.

Sharing Caine's elation that neither her mother nor his brother had proved to be the guilty party, Ivy touched his shoulder in a gesture of affection. He looked up. His smile widened. Without a word he drew her into his arms and buried his face against her neck.

At a muted sound, they drew apart and stared at the hooded, robed figure crossing the room. He hadn't used the front door, but had entered instead from the rear of the cottage. Without even looking around he hurried to the fireplace, stepped up on the hearth and removed the stone from its place in front of the safe. Reaching inside, he removed an envelope, tore it open and stuffed the check beneath the sheet that he had fashioned into a disguise. Then he calmly stepped from the hearth and turned.

Ivy found herself staring down at the figure, straining to find something familiar, something that would identify the blackmailer. She turned to see Caine's reaction. Beside her, Caine's fists clenched at his sides.

The man left quickly the way he had entered, through the back door. As soon as the door clicked shut, Caine stood and helped Ivy to her feet. Together they lowered the ladder and climbed down from the loft.

"Come on." Caine threw open the front door and beckoned her to follow. "We can't let him get away with that check."

There was no longer any reason to hide. With the sun high in the sky, they ran along the curving ribbon of driveway toward the big house on the hill.

Once they were at the house, Caine summoned the butler. "Chester, have any of the cars been taken from the garage?"

The old man shook his head. "The garage is locked, sir. All the cars are in there."

"Good. I want you to make sure that none of those vehicles leaves the grounds. No matter what you have to do. Do you understand?"

The little man's eyes danced. "I knew there was something going on around here. Miss St. Martin's been acting so funny all morning. Is there some trouble, Mr. St. Martin?"

"There could be, Chester. Just see that no one leaves this place until I say so."

"Yes sir." The old man drew himself up to his full five feet four inches and headed for the garage.

"I'm going to find our letter writer, even if I have to search every room in this house," Caine said through gritted teeth. "Let's start with Aunt Gertrude's room. I want to make certain she's all right."

Caine knocked on his aunt's door. There was no sound from within.

"Aunt Trudy. Are you in there?"

Pressing her ear against the door, Ivy muttered. "I hear something. Someone's in there, Caine. Maybe she's been hurt."

"Stand aside, Ivy." Caine's features were contorted with rage. "I'm breaking down this door."

As he threw his shoulder against the door, they could hear the lock turning from inside. Abruptly the door was opened. Gertrude faced them. Tears streamed down her face.

"Oh, Caine." The old woman's face crumpled.

Instantly, he caught her in his arms and held her close. "What is it, Aunt Trudy? Have you been hurt?"

She sobbed for long moments against his chest, then pushed herself away. "I seem to have done more crying this weekend than I have in a lifetime. I haven't been physically hurt, Caine. But the things I've learned today have caused so much pain, as well as joy."

"I don't understand."

She led Caine and Ivy into her bedroom. For long minutes she stared at Ivy, as if really seeing her for the first time. Then she turned to the papers on her desk.

"When I returned from the cottage, these were on my desk. Our blackmailer must have entered my room as soon as I left it, and placed these documents here. Then he went out through the balcony and lowered himself on sheets tied together. Since my room overlooks the woods, he figured no one would see him leaving by this method."

Ivy gasped. "I saw someone on the balcony before breakfast." To Caine, she explained, "I was walking in the woods. I saw something flutter at the balcony. I thought it was one of the maids."

"I suppose he took his luggage down then, so that he could escape as soon as he had the money."

Ivy nodded. "I saw a lot of movement, but by the time I was close enough to see clearly, the figure had disappeared."

Caine's face was grim. "We've probably lost him. He must have left on foot."

"I think you should know something else, Caine." Gertrude held up a familiar-looking slip of paper. "This was shoved under my door a few minutes ago."

Caine and Ivy stared at the check, and then at each other. Their mouths dropped open.

"It seems our blackmailer has had a change of heart."

"But why?"

"I don't know. Maybe he decided my secrets had caused me enough pain through the years. Maybe he just wanted to try something daring." The old woman shrugged. "This has been the strangest day." She turned to Caine. "Before my guests leave, I'd like them all to come to the library."

"Aunt Trudy, you have a right to know who the blackmailer is. We watched him take the check from the safe and put it in his pocket."

"But he has returned my check. That means he isn't really guilty of anything more than revealing to me some facts that have been withheld for a lifetime."

"He sent you threatening letters. He terrorized you. How can you be so quick to overlook what he's done?"

"Because what he has given me is worth far more than any amount of money." She touched his cheek. "Please, Caine, ask everyone to meet me in the library." She gave him an encouraging smile. "Please. I want to talk to Ivy alone for a few minutes."

Caine stared thoughtfully at his aunt, then reluctantly walked from the room. This whole situation just kept getting stranger by the minute.

Ivy entered the library and smiled at the assembled guests before seeking out her mother. Pulling a chair beside Diana, she leaned over and whispered,

"Mother, before Aunt Tru gets here, there's something I have to say."

Diana glanced at the slightly flushed cheeks, the wild tangle of hair to which bits of twigs and leaves still clung. Ivy's eyes, she noted, had the shiny look of fresh tears. But her smile was one of sheer happiness.

"You look like you used to look years ago when you went out climbing trees." She sighed. Her lips curved down in the familiar disapproval. "You were such a tomboy."

"Mother, I know I'll never be quite what you'd hoped for. But despite the fact that I'm a disappointment to you, I want you to know that I love you very much."

Diana's mouth opened, then closed. Tears sprang to her eyes. She blinked, swallowed. "You love me?" Her lips quivered. "After all we've been through?"

Ivy nodded.

"Those are hard words to say." She struggled for composure. "What else did you just say? Not what I'd hoped for?" A tear trickled from the corner of her eye, and she wiped it with a finger, smearing her eye makeup. "How can you even think that? All I'd ever wanted was a little girl. A perfect little girl. And you don't disappoint me. You never did. It's just that I've always wanted so much for you. I want you to have everything."

"But I've always had everything I wanted. I loved growing up here. I had you and Dad. And I have my art. And now I have..."

They both looked up as Gertrude walked briskly into the room. Her gaze swept the familiar faces, before she sat down in a comfortable wingback chair near the fireplace.

The butler closed the double doors, then stood in front of them with his arms crossed firmly over his chest. No one was going to leave this room, unless they walked over him.

"I asked you here because I have some information that I want to share with all of you. I have just been given a wonderful gift."

She glanced over at Ivy, and the young woman gave her a wide smile.

"As you are aware, I was quite a rebellious child. My father never knew quite what to do with me. Of course, looking back, I know that he should have been willing to let me go." Her voice lowered. "I wonder what my life would have been if he had done so." She looked up and caught Judge Tisdale's troubled gaze. "But the old never want to let the young go out on their own, do they? We're always so afraid they'll make a mistake. But that's what life is about, after all. Learning from our mistakes."

She sighed. "Last night, Judge Tisdale mentioned that I quit college to work for a young senator. And he told you that my father, when he heard, flew into a rage and dragged me home to shake some sense into me." She clasped her hands together in her lap. "That's only the beginning of the story. What my father discovered was that I was in love with the young senator, and carrying his child."

Diana gasped. Judge Tisdale sat up very straight. Darren was staring at his prim, maiden aunt as if he'd never really seen her before.

"My father was humiliated. He had no one to turn to for calm advice. He flew into a wild rage. He kept me confined to the house like a prisoner. I was not allowed to communicate with my love. When my time came, he arranged for our family doctor to come to the house to deliver the baby. And when I awoke afterward, my father told me the baby had died." Gertrude's voice cracked. "I smuggled out a note through an elderly maid who was sympathetic. Two weeks later, I heard the news about the senator's death in Central Park. Six weeks later I left for Europe, where I immersed myself in studies at the university for the next four years."

There was no sound in the room, except the crackling of the logs in the fire.

"Today I have been given some documents which prove that my baby didn't die. My father arranged that the baby be adopted by the family who lived on our estate as caretakers. The Murdock family."

Diana's hand flew to her mouth. She started to rise, but Ivy touched her arm. "Please, Mother. Let her finish."

The old woman's voice trembled. "My life has been molded around one painful episode in my youth. Though the sharp pain has dulled, the scar tissue remains. I know I'm a different person than I surely would have been, if I had married my love and raised our son. But look at the lives I've touched because of that one sad event. I had the chance to raise a little sister. I've kept Caine and Darren together. And after a lifetime, I discover a granddaughter. I feel truly blessed."

Gertrude's eyes clouded as she met Diana's questioning stare. "Yes, Diana. Your husband, William, was my son. And I never knew."

"Neither did he," Diana said softly. "Shortly before his death, he found the adoption papers in the safe, along with some old family papers. But when he approached Judge Tisdale about locating his real parents, the judge said the papers had been sealed at the time of the adoption."

"He knew he was adopted?" Ivy asked.

"His family never told him. He only discovered it when he was looking for some insurance papers in the safe. He said it didn't matter," her mother said softly. "The Murdocks had been the only family he had ever known. He loved them."

Gertrude's voice grew stronger. "A part of me is angry that I was denied the chance to love my son. But the best part of this news is that I now have a granddaughter. Ivy." Gertrude's eyes glowed as she looked at the young woman she had always loved.

Stunned at the impact of her words, Diana turned to Ivy. "You knew of this?"

Ivy nodded. Her eyes glistened with tears of happiness. "I just learned of it before I came in here. Aunt Tru wanted to break the news to me upstairs before she faced everyone else." Ivy caught her mother's hand. "Isn't it wonderful?"

Diana blinked back tears of her own. With a catch in her voice, she whispered, "Yes. I know how much you've always loved Gertrude and this old place. Oh, Ivy, your father would have been so proud."

Judge Tisdale cleared his throat. "Gertrude, there's something you should know."

Everyone turned to him. "My grandson came to me with the news of what he had done."

Stunned, the guests grew very quiet as everyone turned to stare at the young lawyer.

"Then it was you, David, who discovered all this?"

As he nodded his head, Gertrude said, "I thought so. What made you decide to return the check?"

"When Diana Murdock came seeking her late husband's birth records, I felt so sorry for her. The answers she sought were there at my fingertips, and I was forbidden to read them. In a moment of weakness, I decided to pursue it further." His voice dropped to nearly a whisper. "But once I'd discovered the truth, an idea began to form." The young man's voice was choked with emotion. "I realize now how much I've abused my privilege as a lawyer. Those papers have been in our family firm for years. And I was willing to violate your privacy, Miss St. Martin, for the sake of money. I knew I wouldn't be able to live with myself if I kept that check."

"And you, Jacob?" Gertrude asked the old man. "Did you know about my baby, too?"

He shook his head. "No, Gertrude. I was just a young lawyer then. The judge who handled the adoption of your baby had the papers sealed. I would never have violated the Murdock right to privacy. And I'm glad I didn't know. It would have been a terrible dilemma, knowing the truth, feeling about you the way I do."

"Would you have had the courage to keep their secret, I wonder? Or would you have given in to the temptation to tell me the truth?"

The old man was solemn. "I'm glad I never had to face that decision. My integrity was never put to the test as David's was."

Gertrude turned to the butler, who looked dazed at the news he had just heard.

"Chester bring some champagne and glasses." To her guests, she said, "I know you have a long way to travel today. But I want you to share in a toast to my newly discovered granddaughter."

Darren came forward to give Ivy a hug. "Does this mean Caine and I won't be her heirs anymore?"

Ivy chuckled. "You're stuck being part of this family forever."

He gave her a wicked grin. "Well, since we're all family now, how about loaning me some money?"

"I still don't have any," Ivy said with a laugh.

"Well, I know where you can get as much as you want," Darren said, glancing at a beaming Gertrude.

"Forget it. Nothing's changed, except that my good friend is now my grandmother."

As he walked past Ivy, David avoided her eyes as he addressed Gertrude. "We'll be going now, Miss St. Martin."

"Not until you join us in a drink, David." Gertrude's voice lowered. "What you did was a terrible thing. But I'm grateful for the information you gave me. And I'm especially glad that you decided to own up to your guilt."

Her eyes met his grandfather's. "It's always difficult to know when the young should be given the responsibility of their own lives. I suppose the deciding factor is when they learn to make difficult choices, regardless of the consequences."

Jacob Tisdale dropped an arm around his grandson's shoulders. "On the ride home, I'd like to talk about retiring. I need some time to relax." As David began to protest, he added, "I've earned that right. Don't argue with me, boy."

David shot Gertrude a grateful look before turning to his grandfather. "Whatever you say."

As Chester passed the champagne, Gertrude lifted her glass. "To truth, no matter how painful." Her eyes misted. "And to my granddaughter, Ivy, who makes me so very proud."

They touched glasses. The old woman's voice grew stronger, as she stared pointedly at Caine and Ivy. "And to love. Without it, there would be no future generations, and thus, no future at all."

Solemnly they drank.

Chapter Eleven

Ivy sat in the sunshine of the terrace, talking quietly with her mother, while Chester brought her luggage downstairs.

"What were you searching for in the attic?" Ivy asked her mother.

"Something from your father's past. I've been thinking of moving away, of making a clean break, and I wanted to close this chapter of my life. I thought his old albums would disclose who his real parents were."

"Is that why you went to see David Tisdale?"

Diana nodded. "They've always handled the Murdock legal work. He easily found the adoption records. But he told me the biological parents' identities must remain a secret. I had decided not to pursue it any further.''

Diana's voice was soft, filled with new expression. ''Every time I look at you, Ivy, I marvel. I was never any good at housework, or child care. While you were growing up, I tried a few part-time jobs. I was never good at anything. And here you are, this brilliant, talented artist. It makes me feel even more of a failure.''

Ivy was stunned. She'd always felt inadequate beside this beautiful woman. It had never occurred to her that her mother had insecurities of her own.

''Mother, don't be silly. You made a loving home for Dad and me. Remember all those beautiful clothes you used to make me?'' She chuckled. ''Of course, on me they always looked like something I'd slept in. But you were a very talented seamstress.''

Diana nodded. ''I've always loved clothes and sewing. That's why I've decided to accept a friend's offer to go to California and work in her dress designing business.''

''Mother. That's wonderful.''

''I'm not fifty yet, Ivy, and I want to try my hand at something before it's too late.''

''You'll be a fabulous designer,'' Ivy said with conviction.

''Will you come and visit me sometime?'' Diana asked almost shyly.

''Of course I will. I'd love to, Mother.''

They hugged each other, then walked arm in arm through the enormous rooms to the front door. There they greeted Gertrude, who had already bade good-bye to Judge Tisdale and his grandson.

"Something just occurred to me, Diana," Gertrude said in her staccato voice. "Since William was my son, you were my daughter-in-law."

Diana laughed. "I'm glad we didn't know that all those years ago, Gertrude. I would have blamed all our troubles on that fact."

The old woman smiled and took her hand. "You are always welcome here, Diana."

"Thank you, Gertrude. I just told Ivy that I'm moving to California. Maybe you'll come with her for a visit."

"I think," the old woman said with a sigh, "that might sound very tempting next winter, when we've been snowed in for months."

"Good. I'll look forward to seeing you."

As Diana walked to her little red sports car, Chester lifted the hood. Just then Caine walked from the house. At the mere sight of him, Ivy felt her heart leap.

Caine looked puzzled. "What's wrong, Chester?"

The old man connected a wire, then closed the hood. "When you told me to keep everyone from leaving, I disabled all their cars. Now I have to make sure they're able to make the trip home."

"Good old Chester," Caine muttered against his aunt's cheek, as he bent to kiss her.

Darren came bounding out the front door, looking better than he had in days.

"I've decided to go back to California and face Melanie with the bitter truth."

"What truth?" Ivy looked into Darren's laughing eyes.

"That the playboy's life is not for me. I'm going to get a job like an ordinary mortal, and try to live a normal life. Without her. I'm not going to contest the divorce."

"You'd better be sure, Darren," Gertrude said firmly. "Love is a very fragile thing. Maybe if you two try to work out your troubles, you'll find the love is even stronger than before."

He bent and kissed his aunt on her cheek. "Aunt Gertrude, I looked at David Tisdale today and saw myself. I think there was a time when I might have been desperate enough to try something foolish in order to get money. I've been in the fast lane too long. Now I'd like to try a slow, easy track."

"Call me," Gertrude said, taking his hand. "Let me know what's happening with you. And Darren, hurry back."

He shook Caine's hand, then grabbed him in a bear hug. "Thanks for everything, big brother. Before you know it, I'll be doing you favors."

"Good. It's about time. I intend to take you up on it."

Darren caught Ivy by the shoulders and held her a little away from him. "And you're still the best looking woman in the county. Next to Aunt Gertrude, of course."

Ivy laughed and pulled his face down for a kiss. "And you're the second best looking man."

"Really? Who beat me out for the title?"

She turned to Caine. "Oh, some funny looking guy I ran into in the dark."

Seeing the look on his brother's face, Darren punched him playfully on the arm. "Better watch out, Caine. I think she's got plans for you."

As Darren's car and Diana's shiny sports car disappeared along the driveway, Chester rolled Ivy's motorcycle from the garage.

"What will I do with this bag, Miss Ivy?"

She took the travel bag from his hand and secured it to the rear of the bike. Picking up her helmet, she walked back to the steps where Gertrude waited.

"It's been quite a birthday, hasn't it?"

The old woman nodded. "In my eighty years, this has been one of the most remarkable times ever."

"I'm not used to calling you Grandma. I may slip and say Aunt Tru."

"Just so you call me often, and let me know how your life is going." She drew the young woman close and hugged her. "Oh, how I wish you could live here. I'm going to miss you so much more now that I know how many years we've lost."

"I'll come back often. Goodbye, Aunt . . . Grandma."

Both women laughed, as they fondly embraced.

Ivy turned to Caine, and found that she couldn't think of a thing to say. They stared at each other for long, awkward moments. Finally, Caine broke the silence.

"I'm leaving too, Aunt Trudy. But I'll be back often. I'm going to start remodeling the cottage soon."

He turned to Ivy, tousling her hair. "So long, Weed. It's been—different. Try to stay out of trouble."

"Yes. You, too." She stared down at her helmet, then pulled it on. "Goodbye, Caine."

She held out her hand and he took it.

Gertrude watched with amusement. "If you two don't mind, I'm feeling rather shaky. I'm going inside for a cup of tea, or something stronger."

"Something stronger, I'm willing to bet," Caine muttered as she made her way inside.

Glancing down at the small hand in his, he ran a thumb over the slender fingers. "Such long, tapered fingers." He thought of those hands on his skin and felt a tightening deep inside.

She withdrew her hand and walked to the motorcycle. *Say you care,* she thought. *Ask me to stay.* She started the bike with a roar, and fastened the strap of her helmet. A glance in Caine's direction assured her he hadn't moved. She hoped the visor of her helmet hid the tears that were stinging her eyes. Engaging the gear, she began to take off in a roar of sound and smoke.

As the bike moved along the curving driveway, rough hands clutched her shoulders. Caine dropped his weight behind her, nearly knocking them both off balance.

She lifted her visor and turned her head slightly. "You could have killed us both. Are you crazy?"

"Yes." The wind whipped away his words. "Ever since I met you, I've become a little bit crazy."

"Where are you going?"

"Wherever you're headed."

"Now I know you're crazy." She gunned the engine, taking the curves with ease.

He held her firmly around the waist, and pressed his lips to her ear. "I used to be normal until I met you."

It was true, he thought. All his life he had known exactly what he wanted. For the first time, nothing mattered except this woman.

They skimmed past the duck pond. Past the woods. Past the clearing. To the cottage.

"Stop here, Ivy."

The sun glinted off the gleaming chrome of the bike. As they dismounted, Caine lifted the helmet from Ivy's head and watched as the familiar dark silk drifted about her face and shoulders.

Taking her hand, he dropped the helmet to the ground and led her to the front door of the cottage. He shoved open the door, then led her inside. She hadn't even been aware that she was crying until this moment.

Strong arms wrapped around her, drawing her against a solid wall of chest. Work-roughened fingers smoothed the tangled hair, and drew her face into the hollow of a warm throat. A voice, deep, vibrant, cooed unintelligible words to her.

She felt his shirt blotting her tears.

"This whole weekend has been overwhelming for you. It's all too much to take in at one time. Your father's adoption. Aunt Tru turning out to be your grandmother."

"And falling in love with you."

The hands at her hair stilled. She heard his sudden intake of breath. He lifted her chin and stared down into her tear-filled eyes.

"Say that again."

The tears spilled over, running down her cheeks. Between sobs, she said, "I love you."

"That's what I thought you said." With his thumbs, he wiped away the tears. His hands cupped the sides of her face. He stared down at her, loving the way her green eyes shimmered.

"I love you, too, Weed."

"Weed." She wiped a hand across her eyes. "Is that any way to address someone you're supposed to love?"

"Ivy, my beautiful little weed."

He rubbed his nose over hers. His lips brushed hers lightly. His voice was so husky, it sent shivers through her. "I love you, Ivy Murdock. And I don't ever want you to leave me."

She kissed him back. "You're never going to get rid of me."

The kiss deepened. He felt the familiar flames leap, then race through his veins, heating his blood, his flesh, his mind.

"Think you could manage to paint in Europe for a little while?"

She struggled to clear her mind. "Europe?"

"I just heard that my European project has been approved. I'll have to spend quite a bit of time there this year."

"I could paint in an underground tunnel, if that's where you had to be."

He grinned and kissed the corners of her eyes. "Hmmm. I might try that. Sounds like fun."

"When will we have to leave?"

"How about right away. We can be married and spend the time in Europe as an extended honeymoon before you have to start work on the mural for the Blayfield Building. And we'll be away from all the family."

"Careful. I just acquired all this family. I'm not sure I want to leave it for too long."

"Don't worry," he said, dragging his lips across her cheek. The heat was growing. He could already feel his control slipping. "Knowing Aunt Trudy, if we stay away too long, she'll find some reason to come visit us. She's a woman with a mind of her own."

Ivy wrapped her arms around his waist, and buried her lips in his throat. Her voice was a sultry whisper against his skin. "I hope you can stand another woman with a mind of her own."

"They're the best kind." He lifted her in his arms and carried her to the loft. Against her lips he murmured, "Let's see if we can finally make love without any interruptions."

"Didn't Aunt Tru say Chester only checks this building once a week?"

"Umm. Yes. Why?"

She laughed and turned her mouth up to his to be kissed. "Then you can count on all the privacy you want." Ivy opened her hand to reveal a shiny key.

"I knew it," he breathed. "That scatterbrained image was all an act. You definitely have a mind of your own."

She chuckled, a warm, sultry sound that whispered across his heart. "Your brother Darren was right. I definitely have plans for his big brother."

Epilogue

Gertrude St. Martin returned from her brisk afternoon stroll and gathered the mail. As she climbed the stairs she sorted through the letters until she came to a plain white envelope. Sitting down on the top step, she dropped the others and tore the letter open, reading quickly.

Europe is wonderful. Feasting on museums and galleries, and of course, architecture.

Of course, the old woman thought with a smile. She could still recall being that young and wildly in love. *All you can see from a hotel window.*

She must plan a party for the newlyweds when they returned from their honeymoon.

Flush from her success as a matchmaker, her mind whirled. Whom could she invite for Darren, now that he was alone? Whom did she know who would love him despite his occasional lapses?

His mate would have to be generous and sweet, with long blond hair and laughing hazel eyes. Yes. Someone like dear Sara.

She stood, and with a girlish gait strode to her sitting room to write the invitations. If she hurried, she might still fill this old house with the laughter of generations.

READERS' COMMENTS ON SILHOUETTE ROMANCES:

"The best time of my day is when I put my children to bed at naptime and sit down to read a Silhouette Romance. Keep up the good work."

P.M.*, Allegan, MI

"I am very fond of the quality of your Silhouette Romances. They are so real. I have tried to read some of the other romances, but I always come back to Silhouette."

C.S., Mechanicsburg, PA

"I feel that Silhouette Books offer a wider choice and/or variety than any of the other romance books available."

R.R., Aberdeen, WA

"I have enjoyed reading Silhouette Romances for many years now. They are light and refreshing. You can always put yourself in the main characters' place, feeling alive and beautiful."

J.M.K., San Antonio, TX

"My boyfriend always teases me about Silhouette Books. He asks me, how's my love life and naturally I say terrific, but I tell him that there is always room for a little more romance from Silhouette."

F.N., Ontario, Canada

*names available on request